HAUNTED BY SIN

TOUCH OF EVIL - BOOK ELEVEN

KENNEDY LAYNE

KENNEDY LAYNE PUBLISHING, INC.

DEDICATION

Jeffrey & Cole — I love you!

About the Book

Revealing the truth could be the key to survival or a catalyst for murder in the next gripping thriller by USA Today Bestselling Author Kennedy Layne...

In three quiet towns across Michigan, a shared name links three women to a chilling fate. Each victim meets a gruesome end, sparking fear and speculation that goes viral on social media. Mary Jane Reynolds, bearing the same name and residing in the same state as the victims, takes matters into her own hands. She posts an online video pleading for the FBI to take the case and give those with the same name protection.

Former FBI profiler Brooklyn Sloane and her team are called in as consultants. While the answers to most investigations are usually discovered with the first murder victim, the profile of this particular case gives Brook reason to believe otherwise. In a shocking revelation, the killer's fixation might not be on the name itself.

As the investigation unfolds, an unsettling theory begins to emerge—the reason behind the murders is most likely due to

ABOUT THE BOOK

a shared secret that not even the victims know binds them together. Will exposing the truth save lives, or will doing so become the catalyst for something far worse?

CONTENTS

CHAPTER ONE

Brooklyn Walsh

June 1996

Tuesday — 10:47 am

CAREFREE LAUGHTER FLOATED AROUND the campsite, punctuated by the occasional shriek of excitement from those enjoying the summer camp's activities. Most of the children darted between chaotic craft tables and challenging obstacle courses with the encouragement of their counselors. Other groups had gathered to play games in the open field between the cabins. There was no denying the bustling energy from those in attendance.

"Just get the frisbee, Brook," Sally complained as she shielded her eyes from the sun. She rested her other hand on her hip in impatience. "It couldn't have gone that far into the woods."

Brook wasn't afraid of the woods so much as she was of poison ivy. She had practically been covered with the itching rash from head to toe last year. She had also missed out on several fun events because of her horrible reaction, and she didn't plan for that to happen this summer. She peered over her shoulder, hoping to spot her brother.

Jacob wasn't afraid of anything.

"Brook, hurry up!"

"Fine," Brook muttered to herself when she couldn't locate Jacob. She thought she had spotted him earlier near the water jugs, but he was nowhere in sight. She raised her voice to answer Sally. "I'm going!"

Brook scrunched her nose before somehow summoning the courage to cross the tree line. The overhead leaves provided instant shade. Pockets of sunlight filtered through the branches, and the scent of sunblock had been quickly overpowered by the earthy, damp odor of the forest floor. The humidity was so thick that Brook held her arms up so that her shirt wouldn't be left with wet stains on the fabric.

She walked gingerly in the direction where the frisbee must have fallen after bouncing off one of the trees, but the disc was nowhere to be found. The hard plastic was red, so it should have been easy to spot. The entire time she canvassed the area, she kept a very close eye on any green leaves that resembled poison ivy. She had been so engrossed by the foliage that she hadn't realized the ground sloped downward until it was too late.

The soles of Brook's running shoes were no match for the steep terrain, and she lost her footing. Unable to catch herself, her hands were of no use to her as they were scraped by small twigs and debris all the way down to the bottom of the small ravine.

"Great," Brook muttered in frustration as she remained on the ground to take stock of her injuries.

There were several scratches on her hands. Upon closer inspection, they didn't seem too deep. She blinked away her tears and wiped her palms on her shorts before she scanned her surroundings. This part of the woods always made her uneasy.

It was quiet...too quiet.

Until she heard an odd fluttering to her left. She quickly turned to find a male cardinal sitting on a low-hanging branch.

His feathers were the same color as her frisbee. The bird stared at her for a while before he flittered away, as if to remind her that she should be moving as well. All she wanted to do was find her frisbee as fast as possible so that she could get back to the game with her friends.

A twig snapped, causing Brook to startle.

No bird was heavy enough to make that type of sound.

"What are you doing here?"

Brook scrambled to her feet upon hearing the question. A girl with long blonde hair stood between two large trees. She wore a purple shirt with the name "Stella" glued to the front of the fabric with shimmering glitter.

"I'm looking for my frisbee," Brook replied as she brushed the dirt off her shorts. She studied Stella, guessing the girl to be about the same age as Jacob. "You don't go to my summer camp. Are you out here with your family?"

At first, Brook had been relieved that someone else was in the woods. She didn't like the quiet. Neither had the cardinal. Right now, there weren't any birds chirping. Her mother always said that usually meant they were scared.

"Campers have to stay inside the boundary. Aren't those the rules?"

"Yes," Brook said with a frown. She didn't like the girl's tone. "You don't have to be so mean."

"This is my spot, and I don't want you here." Stella crossed her arms and continued to stare at Brook. "If you were shipped off to summer camp, then your parents didn't want you, either."

"That's not true!"

"Are you sure about that?" Stella taunted with an evil smile. "How long is that summer camp, anyway? One week? Two?"

"Stella!" A man's voice called from a distance. "Where are you?"

"I'm coming!" Stella shouted over her shoulder. She turned back to Brook with a snotty expression. "You better leave. And don't come to my spot again."

Before Brook could respond, Stella disappeared into the dense foliage. The leaves rustled and snapped as the girl ran away. She hadn't been very nice. Brook's mother would have scolded Stella for not being kind to others.

Not wanting to get into trouble for being gone from camp for too long, Brook made her way back up the slight incline. She had to grab onto a few branches for leverage, but she finally managed to reach the top without slipping or hopefully rubbing against any poison ivy.

A bright flash of red caught her eye.

There was her frisbee, sitting right at the base of a nearby tree. Brook smiled in victory as she quickly grabbed it. A part of her thought that maybe Stella had hidden the disc on purpose. Some kids weren't nice, and she obviously fell into that category.

"Rude," Brook whispered to herself as she made her way back to camp.

Brook couldn't understand why anyone would think summer camp was a bad place. There were a ton of fun games to play, crackling campfires to sit around in the evening, and gooey s'mores that were delicious. The counselors made everything fun, so maybe Stella was just jealous.

As Brook broke through the tree line, she was greeted by the sight of Sally performing a cartwheel. Before too long, others were following suit and grading one another on their landings. The sounds of laughter once again overtook the area, and everything had gone back to normal. Brook smiled as she ran to join her friends, and the sting of Stella's hurtful words faded away into nothing but a hazy memory.

CHAPTER TWO

Brooklyn Sloane

May 2024

Thursday — 10:08 am

THE SMOOTH, STEADY PURR of the SUV's tires created a comforting rhythm against the freshly laid asphalt. The vibrant scenery of the highway was nothing but a blur of mixed greens and blues, framed by the tinted windows that kept the sun's rays at bay. No one could have asked for a more beautiful May day—not too hot to be uncomfortable, but not too cold to require coats.

Unfortunately, the perfect weather brought to mind Stella Bennett and the summer of 1996. The theories surrounding the girl's disappearance were something that Brook could do without this morning.

She glanced toward the map on the infotainment display. According to the directions listed on the left-hand side of the screen, they were still many miles away from their exit. She pressed the cruise control button so that she could stretch her legs.

"Do you think it was a dream or a memory?" Sylvie Deering asked from the passenger side seat. She had exchanged her usual, black-rimmed glasses for a pair of oversized prescription sunglasses. Her blonde hair was pulled back in its usual bun, but some of the strands had escaped to frame the right side of her face. No one would ever have guessed that she had a brush with death three months ago. "I mean, it wouldn't be a stretch to assume you buried a lot of unpleasant memories from back then."

"I wish I knew the answer," Brook responded truthfully as she rubbed her left thigh. She had run for an additional mile during her morning jog before being driven to the airport. She had been distracted by the possible direction the search could go for Stella Bennett's remains. "There is a good chance it was both a dream and a memory. We know that Stella was with her uncle during that summer, and we know their campsite wasn't too far from the location of my summer camp. I could have seen Stella from a distance. I could have spoken to her. Or...my mind is trying to fill in the blanks."

"You would think with what we see on a daily basis that it wouldn't surprise me a boy so young could commit murder." Sylvie closed the lid of her laptop, which she had been using to research their most recent case that had nothing to do with Stella Bennett. The hot spot on Sylvie's phone had provided an adequate signal strength for the most part. "If Stella was Jacob's first victim, he would have only been eleven years old when he killed her."

By all intents and purposes, Jacob Matthew Walsh had been a sweet boy raised by two loving parents in a quiet suburban neighborhood. Before that fateful summer, he had been surrounded by friends, played football, and doted on his baby sister. He had been...normal.

Or so Brook had thought at the time.

The mind was a fickle thing when it came to drawing conclusions, and she wasn't so sure there was any credibility to her memories. The one hard truth Brook couldn't deny was that her brother was a serial killer.

"I spoke to the federal agent leading the grid search, and he's going to concentrate on the campground in the coming weeks." Brook checked her rearview mirror out of habit. Since it was well past the morning rush hour, there weren't that many vehicles on the highway. "The search team has been focused on the site where Stella's uncle set up camp back then, but what if Jacob somehow managed to drag Stella's body back to a setting where he was most comfortable? It's worth checking out."

Brook noticed immediately when Sylvie straightened her shoulders and rested a hand over her abdomen. It was as if she had suddenly experienced a sharp pain. She hadn't complained once during her recovery, and her most recent doctor appointment had provided her an all-clear for field duty. Such official clearance didn't mean that Brook wouldn't keep a close eye on Sylvie in the coming weeks.

"I'm fine, you know," Sylvie muttered in displeasure as she reached for her computer bag behind Brook's seat. "I don't want to be handled with kid gloves, Brook. I'm in better shape now than before the attack."

Brook believed Sylvie's statement to be accurate, but only in the physical sense. Her mental well-being was for another discussion altogether.

There wasn't one aspect of Brook's life that hadn't been stained by her brother's sins. While Jacob was currently behind bars in federal prison, he had still managed to set plans in motion that would secure his freedom. One of those plans had backfired recently, and Sylvie had been on the receiving end of an attack by one of Jacob's unhinged followers.

For that matter, so had Brook.

She forced herself to stop massaging her left thigh before Sylvie could turn the conversation to Brook's own recovery. The scar tissue was still tender and angry beneath her fingers, and there was no denying that the blade of the knife had severed more nerves than she had originally thought. She still found herself waking up in the middle of the night from the sharp, burning pain, which meant Sylvie experienced the same on a nightly basis...or worse.

The ringing of Brook's phone emanated from the speaker system of the SUV. She had connected her phone to the vehicle's Bluetooth, so she was able to answer with a press of the button on the steering wheel.

"Sloane."

"This is Special Agent Rick Tirelli." The federal agent's deep voice contained a slight Boston accent, but the phone number on the display had a Michigan area code. "Listen, you might want to reschedule your morning plans. There are media vans parked in front of Mary Jane Reynolds' house. Two local, and one national. It wouldn't surprise me if more camera crews are on the way after her video went viral yesterday."

It was clear from Agent Tirelli's tone that he didn't appreciate the way Miss Reynolds had handled her situation, but fear was a powerful motivator. The woman should be afforded some leeway, especially given that three other women with the same name had lost their lives in what could only be described as gruesome deaths.

"Are you at Miss Reynolds' residence right now, Agent Tirelli?"

"No. One of the local deputies gave me a heads up."

"While I appreciate the warning, my colleague and I will keep the appointment we have scheduled with Miss Reynolds," Brook replied as she turned off the vehicle's cruise control. She pressed the gas pedal so as not to lose speed while activating her turn signal. Their exit was just up ahead. "I'll keep you apprised of the meeting, as well as provide you with an address as to where my team and I will be staying for the time being."

"Don't say I didn't warn you, Sloane."

Brook's previous experience as a former federal profiler hadn't seen her in the field often, but that had changed drastically when she handed in her resignation years ago. She was now part owner and operator of S&E Investigations, Inc. The private investigative firm had not initially been set up to consult on serial cases for the Bureau, but the direction of the firm had been altered early on in the firm's infancy.

The offices of S&E Investigations were located in Washington, D.C., and the firm employed several other team members who had become like family to Brook over the years. Considering that she had basically isolated herself from everyone to concentrate on hunting her brother, it spoke a lot to her colleagues' characters that she viewed life differently now.

"Do you know him?" Sylvie asked about Agent Tirelli after Brook had disconnected the call. Sylvie fastened the flap of her laptop bag before lifting it over the middle console to store it in the backseat. "Personally, I mean?"

"No." Brook eased off the gas as she guided the SUV toward the exit. "I read Agent Tirelli's file on the flight here, though. He seems to be a solid agent. He is merely a point of contact. We have full reign over the investigation."

Brook gently pressed on the brake pedal, bringing the vehicle to a smooth stop at the intersection. She had turned off the annoying voice programmed into the GPS, but the directions were clearly instructing her to turn left. She had a different plan in mind. The gas station on the right side of the highway not only promised a quick break for both herself and Sylvie but also the ability to make contact with Theo and Bit.

Theo Neville and Bobby 'Bit' Nowacki were driving the firm's Mercedes Sprinter Technical Van outfitted with everything the firm would need while in the field. Bit was the firm's tech specialist, and he had spent months putting together a mobile office with top-of-the-line surveillance equipment. The van had been a game-changer for the team when on field assignments.

Whereas Theo and Sylvie were both former federal agents, Bit had learned everything in his specialty through life experiences. Not all of them had been on the right side of the law, either. Brook couldn't pass judgment considering the extreme measures she had taken over the years in her search for Jacob.

"Go ahead and use the restroom," Brook instructed as she deftly pulled the SUV parallel to a gas pump before cutting the engine. "I'll top off the tank."

Brook unfastened her seat belt before grabbing her cell phone. The corporate credit card she needed to purchase fuel was in the sleeve of her phone case. By the time she had swiped her card, removed the gas cap, and inserted the nozzle into the gas tank opening, Sylvie was already inside the convenience store. Brook took advantage of her time alone and accessed her speed dial list. She pressed her thumb firmly on the second name listed on the display.

"We're so switching places next time," Theo said in irritation without any preamble. "This entire van smells like onions, and we've only been on the road for the past hour."

"Hey, Boss!"

Brook ignored the sideways glare she received from the male subject on the other side of the pump. She was well aware that she shouldn't be on her cell phone while pumping gas. Pulling on the handle, she opened the driver's side door and climbed in behind the steering wheel. The SUV had a large fuel tank, and she could monitor the intake from her seat.

"Sylvie is doing just fine," Brook stated, answering the unspoken question from both Theo and Bit. They were both worried about Sylvie, and their concern was very valid. "We're at a gas station, maybe eight miles from Mary Jane Reynolds' neighborhood."

"I'm switching to video," Theo advised, prompting Brook to pull the phone away from her ear. Theo's face suddenly came into view, and his position in the passenger seat told her that Bit was driving the van. No wonder Theo wasn't in the best of moods. "Arden is all set to pick up the kitten this weekend."

Arden Hinnish was a former private investigator who manned the offices of S&E Investigations when the team was called out into the field. At sixty-eight years of age, his experience offered a different perspective, albeit a welcome one. He had also become a father figure to those at the firm, and it had been his idea that had put the entire pet idea into motion.

"We have no idea how long this investigation will take," Brook pointed out as she sat sideways in the seat. The tank was only half full. In her opinion, so was the plan to pick out a kitten without Sylvie's knowledge. "We could be here for weeks, Theo."

Brook understood that the team wanted to ensure Sylvie was okay after losing her father to pancreatic cancer. She had also mentioned several times that she wanted a kitten to come home to after working the types of caseloads the firm dealt with daily, but the travel involved was an obstacle that couldn't be overlooked.

"Arden has already declared himself the uncle of said furball, and he already has plans in place to take the kitten home with him when we're required to travel out of the city." Theo readjusted his hold on the phone so that Brook had a better view of his good eye. The black patch covering his right eye had been the result of an injury sustained in the field during his tenure with the Bureau. In her opinion, the impairment caused others to underestimate his abilities. "Sylvie needs this, Brook."

Considering that Brook didn't always read certain situations correctly when it came to others' personal lives, she had made the conscious decision to leave it in the hands of the others. She wouldn't change her mind now, which was why she chose to change the subject.

"Fine," Brook muttered as she stepped out of the SUV. "Hold on a second."

She set her cell phone in the seat so that she could remove the nozzle and replace the gas cap. The male subject across from her was now using the squeegee to clean his windows, and Brook didn't want him to hear the rest of the conversation. Once she had taken the receipt and stored it on the side of the door for safekeeping, she picked up the phone to reclaim her seat.

"...too close. If the guy brakes, we're going to..." Theo was now holding the phone with one hand while resting his palm on the ceiling of the van with the other. "Bit, go around him. Do you want me to drive? I can..."

Brook spotted Sylvie walking back toward the SUV. She was casually scanning those individuals standing at the gas pumps, but there was also an alertness in her body language that hadn't been there before her attack.

"Is there anything that Sylvie and I should know before we meet with Mary Jane Reynolds?" Brook asked as she guided their conversation toward the case. "Agent Tirelli called a little while ago to inform us that her video had done its job. The press is already camped out in front of her house."

"I just received the file on the third victim," Theo replied right as Sylvie opened the passenger side door. She hoisted herself into the seat with ease. "I've also put in a request for the local authorities to send all evidence to our forensics lab for retesting. I've designated the chain of emails numerically so there won't be any confusion."

"Did you know that there are over four thousand Mary Jane Reynolds in the country?" Bit chimed in, much to Theo's dismay if his expression was anything to go by. He muttered something about paying attention to the road, but Bit must have caught sight of the screen. "Hey, Little T! Gumshoe found us a rental on a lake. He'll be sending you the address shortly."

Bit's propensity for nicknames was endearing unless he didn't like someone. Fortunately for the team, he had given them accurate monikers. While Bit referred to Theo as Big T due to the man's muscular frame, Sylvie's was Little T for her love of tea. Gumshoe was simply an old reference to what people used to call private investigators back in the day, and it suited Arden perfectly. As for Brook's nickname, only Bit was able to get away with calling her Boss. She didn't view herself as such, because they all contributed their talents equally to their cases.

"I'll start drafting a profile of the unsub once we set up shop at the rental tonight," Brook said with a hint of annoyance. She didn't like working out of sync, but this case wasn't a typical serial investigation. "I ed what files Arden was able to upload into our software system. On the surface, the two common denominators between the victims are their names and their state of residence."

"Mary Jane Reynolds." Sylvie had also read over the uploaded reports on their flight to Michigan, and her memory was close to eidetic. "All three Mary Janes were stabbed to death. Mary One was murdered last October at her residence in Ann Arbor. Mary Two was killed inside her home located in a neighborhood outside of Lansing this past January. And Mary Three's body was discovered on the side of a jogging trail near her parents' home in Mount Pleasant last month. Brook has her work cut out for her on the profile due to several factors. The unsub doesn't seem to care about race, age, profession, physical attributes, or even societal classes. Basically, we are left with no pattern except for the method of killing."

The root of the problem lay in the fact that these three murders were now inextricably tied together by the powerful influence of social media. All it had taken was one person to post a comment in a thread regarding the odd coincidence of the names to spark a ton of conspiracy theories. The local police in each of the cities had been working tirelessly to solve their individual cases, but they didn't have the manpower needed to form a task force. Now that a third victim with the same name and cause of death had emerged, the FBI had been forced to act quickly, especially given the most recent scrutiny.

"Maybe you should let Theo drive for a while, Bit," Brook suggested much to Theo's apparent relief. "You can start to create an application that compares the victims' information side by side as we collect data. There must be similarities between the victims that were overlooked at first glance."

"We'll start by interviewing Mary Four," Sylvie advised Theo and Bit as she reached for her seat belt.

"Why are we giving Mary Four a number?" Bit asked over the sound of his blinker. He was taking Brook's advice, which had prompted Theo to remove his hand from the ceiling overhead. "She's not dead yet. Plus, she took advantage of her name to gain notoriety on social media. How do we even know we're in the right town to solve this case? The killer could easily still be in Mount Pleasant. Not to mention that there are still sixteen other women listed as potential victims."

While Bit's observation about Mary Jane Reynolds' video being a blatant grab for fame was not wrong, it only scratched the true extent of the situation. The woman's plea for protection had gone viral, spreading like wildfire across the internet. No one could blame the woman for living in fear, but she had also inadvertently placed herself in danger.

Mary Jane had also managed to put several law enforcement agencies under the microscope of the public eye. While no detective involved was completely convinced the three murders were related other than by mere coincidence, the FBI was unwilling to risk their reputation being tarnished. S&E Investigations, known for their high success rate in complicated cases like these, had been brought on in a desperate attempt to appease the public and quell their fears.

Brook didn't care for the firm being used as a public relations stunt, which was why she intended to solve all three deaths...whether or not the team was dealing with one killer or three.

"Unfortunately, we *don't* know if we're in the right area to solve this case, Bit." Brook paused and shared a knowing glance with Sylvie. They had already spoken at length about the investigation on the drive from the airport, both coming to the same conclusion. "But if the unsub had no prior knowledge regarding Mary Jane Reynolds' existence—Mary Four, in this case—he certainly does now."

CHAPTER THREE

Brooklyn Sloane

May 2024

Thursday — 10:32 am

THE QUIET SUBURB OF Crestlake, Michigan had been transformed into a hive of activity. The middle-class neighborhood was made up of cookie-cutter homes, all of which had pristine lawns, colorful flowerbeds, and perfectly pruned hedges. While it was possible that the residents might have ignored something slightly amiss in their sheltered environment, it would have been impossible to overlook the commotion taking place right outside one particular home.

The white picket fence surrounding the two-story house should have signaled domestic tranquility, but it now served as a barrier against the press and onlookers who buzzed with morbid curiosity. Neighbors were clustered together on the sidewalk, their expressions a mixture of curiosity and trepidation. A young woman in leggings and an oversized sweatshirt stood on the sidewalk and spoke with a local reporter. Her hands fluttered

like distressed birds as she spoke animatedly about the individual in question—Mary Jane Reynolds.

"Looks like a block party," Sylvie murmured as she fixed her
gaze on the scene ahead. She raised her cell phone and began to
capture screenshots of the spectacle. In their line of work, details mattered, and sometimes those details were lurking in the
crowd. "You realize that you're going to have to give a statement,
right?"

"I really dislike being put on display as some sort of PR stunt,"
Brook stressed her displeasure, well aware that she would need
to give a statement to the press. S&E Investigations had become
the face of this investigation. The FBI didn't want to waste time
or resources if these cases turned out not to be connected,
and they were more than willing to pay to make the problem
go away. "I guarantee that Agent Tirelli was instructed by his
supervisor to steer clear of the area."

"Well, at least he was nice enough to give you a heads up,"
Sylvie pointed out as she tucked her phone into the side pocket
of her purse. She kept her sunglasses on instead of exchanging
them with her usual, black-rimmed glasses. "I don't see any of
the local police parked in the neighborhood. I'll place a call to
the sheriff to make sure he keeps a deputy in the area until we
have more answers. Ready?"

Brook had parked a few houses down from their intended
destination to give herself time to study their surroundings.
The theatrical performance playing out in front of Mary Jane
Reynolds' residence didn't seem to bother the woman. Otherwise, she would have closed the curtains on her front windows.
Every now and then, someone inside the home would pass by
the windowpane. His or her presence would inevitably be a
trigger for the cameramen to shift their focus.

"No," Brook muttered in response to the question. She shoul-
dered open her door anyway. She slipped her phone into her
purse before she stepped out of the SUV. Once Sylvie had done

the same, Brook pressed the lock button to secure the vehicle. She hid the wince in response to the loud beep capturing every-one's attention. "Sylvie, walk on the inside."

Sylvie parted her lips as if to argue, but the resounding voices of excitement seemed to have changed her mind. She gave a curt nod before joining Brook on the sidewalk. They didn't have to stroll far before the frenzied media had created a barrier between them and the gate of the white picket fence.

"Can you believe it?" someone whispered over the snapping shutters of cameras and the questions being hurled from the reporters. "Right here in our own backyard..."

The reporters began their own line of questioning.

"...is Mary Jane Reynolds the killer's next target?"

"Will the FBI provide every Mary Jane Reynolds in the state of Michigan with a security detail, or will..."

Brook held up her hand to stop the flow of inquiries.

"Please, if you would allow me to speak, I'll give you a brief statement for your noon segment."

Brook's voice sliced through the clamor with an authorita-tive clarity. Microphones immediately raised like an array of metallic flowers reaching for the sun. A vibrating hush finally descended over the crowd.

"As of yesterday, S&E Investigations has officially been re-tained by the Bureau to assist in the investigations involving three victims all named Mary Jane Reynolds," Brook announced, though she doubted the information came as a shock to the press. The FBI had already put out a statement to such effect. "Due to the ongoing nature of these cases, we won't be providing any specifics at this time. However, I assure you that we are fully committed to uncovering the truth. As you all know, the FBI val-ues the role of the press in keeping the public informed, which means that when we have something to share with you, my firm will either issue a press release or request a press conference. In the meantime, we would appreciate your cooperation in maintaining the integrity of this ongoing investigation."

Brook paused, allowing her last sentence to not only resonate with the members of the press but also serve as an exit strategy. A murmur rippled through the crowd, and while some of the reporters continued to eagerly toss out questions, the majority seemed to understand that she would say no more on the subject matter. Upon hearing Jacob's name in one of the numerous inquiries, Brook merely arched her brow and let her expression convey her opinion of such a personal question as she began to advance, forcing the audience to part.

"That was very well done," Sylvie murmured as Brook lifted the small handle on the white gate. Once they were through and the latch was secured behind them, they began to walk down the narrow path to Mary Jane Reynolds' front door. "You spoke efficiently, but somehow managed to say absolutely nothing."

Brook took the compliment as she studied their surroundings, wanting to know everything and anything about Mary Jane Reynolds. According to the woman's background check, she worked in retail at a very exclusive boutique in town. She was in her late twenties, single, and rented the two-story home from one of her family members for half of what rent would normally cost her in this neighborhood.

The front door had been painted a vibrant, cheerful yellow, offset by immaculate white trim. A wreath adorned the entrance with scores of daisies and lush green leaves. The decoration hung delicately from a brass holder, welcoming visitors with its beauty.

"It's all staged," Brook noted quietly as her gaze settled on the welcome mat. The images of daisies were woven in between the letters to keep with the porch's theme. "Mary Jane posted a video last month to share with her followers how to make this very wreath."

Mary Jane was all about being an influencer. Every single day for the past year, she made sure to post perfectly polished reels on social media. It was all about fashion, makeup, home décor, and those recipes that made one's mouth water. She had a decent number of followers, but it wasn't until she posted the video about the three victims who shared her name that things really blew up for her.

Suddenly, she had become viral famous.

Before Brook could lift her hand to knock, the door swung inward. Mary Jane stood framed in the entrance with a small smile on her face. She held the door open just wide enough to cause a stir from those outside wanting to capture some footage. It was difficult to determine if she relished the attention.

"Miss Reynolds, I'm Brooklyn Sloane with S&E Investigations." Brook gestured toward Sylvie. "This is my colleague, Sylvie Deering. As I explained on the phone earlier this morning, our firm has been retained by the Bureau to investigate your concerns regarding the three victims who share your name."

Mary Jane was a beautiful woman. Her long brown hair had hints of auburn highlights, adding depth and dimension to the strands. Her green eyes were framed by thick, dark lashes that were a result of premium products. Delicate lines of eyeliner and shimmery eyeshadow complemented her skin tone, and the rest of her makeup had been meticulously applied, leaving her complexion flawless and radiant.

She was meant to be in the spotlight.

"Please, come in." Mary Jane extended the invitation as she stepped back, making room for Brook and Sylvie to cross the threshold. It didn't go unnoticed that she kept the door ajar long enough for prying lenses to steal glances at the interior. The lime green vase with orange flowers set on an antique piece of furniture would undoubtedly be featured online sometime soon. "I'm so glad that the FBI is now taking this threat seriously. If it took my video to get the job done, then so be it."

Mary Jane finally closed the door before stepping around Brook and Sylvie. The scent of her perfume was faint, but that might have been due to the plug-in air fresheners in almost every outlet. The strawberry fragrance was quite heavy as Mary Jane led Brook and Sylvie into the living room. Brook cleared her throat as she continued to read between the lines.

"This is my fiancé, Adam Bouras." Mary Jane introduced a man who was standing near the window, though he was far enough away to avoid being captured on film. He stepped forward and shook their hands. "And this is Cindy, my sister."

Cindy resembled Mary Jane, though the woman's hair was shorter with blonde highlights. Her smile didn't reach her eyes, and she seemed to be genuinely concerned for her sister.

"It's good to see that you're surrounding yourself with people," Brook pointed out as she took a seat on the couch. Sylvie joined her, setting her purse on the hardwood floor. "With all the attention you're receiving, you've been thrust into the limelight. It could take some time for the curiosity to fade."

The living room was just as bright and cheery as the exterior of the house. Natural light poured in through the large windows, illuminating the soft cream paint on the walls. Bright pops of color in the form of vibrant throw pillows and artful decorations spoke of Mary Jane's talent to blend décor seamlessly.

"I'm scared," Mary Jane stated bluntly as she took a seat in the overstuffed chair. Her fiancé had left his position near the window to stand next to her. His black hair was slicked back, and there was no denying the man's attractiveness. When he placed his hand on Mary Jane's shoulder, she reached up and laced her fingers with his. "I mean, it's obvious that I'm a target based on my name. I could be next."

"Which is why your video plea was a bold move," Brook responded truthfully, not seeing the need to sugarcoat the situation. "Miss Reynolds, while there have been three murders committed over the past seven months of women sharing your name, the police have yet to connect the cases with any substantial evidence. If the investigations are unrelated, you have nothing to worry about. If, however, we do find that the women were linked in some other manner or through DNA left at the crime scenes, then you've made yourself a target."

"I had to do something," Mary Jane responded as she tilted her chin defiantly. "I couldn't just sit here and wait to be killed by some lunatic with a knife."

"Didn't you say that the FBI hired you?" Adam asked as he slipped his free hand into the pocket of his khaki pants. "It's pretty obvious that the cases are connected, right? You wouldn't be here otherwise."

"Until we receive a forensics report comparing the DNA at each crime scene, we're looking into all possibilities," Sylvie responded as she rested her hands on her knees. "Are you staying with Miss Reynolds, Mr. Bouras?"

"Adam, please. And no, I travel a lot for work. I'm an insurance adjuster."

"I'm staying with my sister for the time being," Cindy offered up from her spot near the television. She had her phone in her hand, and she had been switching her attention between the screen and them. "We both work at the boutique, so we just made sure our schedules aligned."

"That's good to know," Brook said before getting right down to it. "Miss Reynolds, I'd like to ask you some questions."

"You can call me Mary Jane."

"Mary Jane," Brook said in concession. "Did you know the victims personally?"

"No," Mary Jane responded as she finally released her fiancé's hand. "None of them."

"Not even from social media?" Brook pressed for clarification.

"Not that I know of," Mary Jane responded with a sideways glance toward her sister. "Cindy?"

"I don't think so, but you're now up to..." Cindy paused to access information on her phone. "Two million, one hundred, and six thousand followers. I suppose we could do a search for your name. I never thought of that."

"Cindy, do you help handle your sister's social media?"

"I couldn't do it without Cindy's help," Mary Jane interjected with what appeared to be sincere appreciation. "She helps with the lighting, the editing, and scheduling of all my posts."

Cindy's fingers were currently typing away on her phone.

"Mary Jane, have you noticed anything out of the ordinary lately?" Brook asked, not concerned in the least that something would be overlooked during today's meeting. Sylvie would ensure that all the details were uploaded into the firm's shared software program. "A car parked outside of your home? Someone outside your place of business who shouldn't be there? Unusual phone calls?"

"No. Nothing like that." Something must have jarred Mary Jane's memory. She frowned before glancing up at her fiancé. "Adam? There was that incident at the bar last weekend."

"Bar?" Brook asked, hoping for more clarification.

"We like to go to either the Crestlake Bar & Grill on the pier or the local pub in town on the weekends. Sometimes on a Thursday, too. Both are local hangout spots. Fun ones, too," Mary Jane replied as she refocused her attention on Brook. "Crestlake Bar & Grill is an outdoor establishment located on one of the piers west of town. The place is relatively upscale for a seasonal stomping ground, so I wasn't expecting some guy to make a scene."

"The guy was drunk, MJ." Adam crossed his arms and widened his stance. He addressed Brook and Sylvie with the rest of his response. "We went out last Saturday night. Some guy couldn't hold his liquor, and he was hitting on every woman in the place. A friend and I made sure he was escorted to the parking lot."

Sylvie confirmed the name of the establishment before following up with more questions about their daily, weekly, and monthly routine. Brook kept an eye on Cindy, who had interrupted to say that there were three followers named Mary Jane Reynolds. The team was already aware of those three individuals, but there was no need to point that out. Those particular women just so happened to live in different states.

"Mr. Bouras, did you know any of the victims?" Brook asked, widening the circle. "You mentioned that you travel a lot for your job. Could the victims be clients of your company?"

"I didn't know the other women," Adam replied before recognition hit. "Are you suggesting that I—"

"No, I'm not suggesting anything," Brook reassured him as she pulled out a business card that she had tucked in the pocket of her blazer. "We're merely trying to establish a connection. Locating a starting point is critical to connecting the investigations. As far as we are aware, the victims didn't know one another. The few similarities we have found are weak, such as two of the women liked to cook and followed some of the same groups on social media. Two enjoyed frequenting wineries, two were into jogging, two preferred cats over dogs, and two were avid readers. All different correlations, leading us back to square one."

"I prefer Pilates, love wine, don't have pets, and I tend to stream movies and shows over reading," Mary Jane offered up with a slight shrug. She rubbed her chest subconsciously, causing the material of her blouse to shift with the motion. "I know you probably think that I only posted that video to get more followers, but I'm honestly terrified that someone might try to kill me. You said it yourself—three women named Mary Jane Reynolds have been murdered in the past seven months. What if this psychopath doesn't like the name Mary Jane Reynolds? What if he has a hit list and is working his way across the state? The country?"

Brook had already drawn the conclusion that Mary Jane was truly frightened for her life. It was also evident that she didn't mind the benefits that came along with posting said video. Whether the publicity made the team's job easier or more difficult remained to be seen.

The next twenty minutes were spent discussing potential security measures that Mary Jane could implement into her daily and nightly routines. Brook also emphasized that additional patrols in the neighborhood were not a guaranteed solution but could serve as a deterrent. Brook assured Mary Jane that they would keep her updated on the progress of the investigation, as well.

"In the meantime, please reach out to me if you can think of anything odd that has occurred over the past couple of weeks," Brook said as she gestured toward the business card that she had placed on the coffee table. "The same goes for you, Mr. Bouras and Miss Reynolds."

Brook had included both Mary Jane's fiancé and sister in the request. They both nodded their agreement as Brook and Sylvie stood to take their leave. Brook could sense the vibrations coming from her phone, but she made no move to answer the call. As Mary Jane guided them toward the front door, a framed document on the wall in the middle of several framed photographs caught Brook's attention.

She remained silent until she and Sylvie had made their way through the throng of reporters. It appeared as if most of the neighbors had made their way back inside their homes. The camera crews were still hoping the viral sensationalist would emerge from her residence to make a formal statement.

"Mary Jane Reynolds is adopted," Brook announced as she closed the driver's side door. The interior of the SUV had warmed up comfortably from the morning sun. "There was a framed certificate on her wall, along with family photographs. Considering that Cindy resembles her sister and she was also in the pictures celebrating the event, it stands to reason that the two of them were adopted by the same parents."

"Mary One was adopted." Sylvie tucked her purse on the floor before retrieving her cell phone. "I'll check on the other two victims. Maybe we missed something. It would be nice to catch a break this early in the case."

Brook agreed with Sylvie's sentiment, but they technically already had a fortunate insight regarding a pattern in the investigation. Should the murders turn out to be connected, there were approximately three months in between each killing. Such calculations left the team with a mere two months to track down and capture the unsub before another innocent life was taken.

CHAPTER FOUR

Brooklyn Sloane

May 2024

Thursday — 6:57 pm

THE EVENING AIR AT the pier was cool and refreshing, unlike the heavy humidity that probably settled over the area in the summertime. A gentle breeze carried the enticing scents of fried seafood and sun-warmed wood, causing one's stomach to rumble in anticipation of a good meal. It was the stunning view that made for a perfect evening—the way the sun hung low in the sky, casting a golden glow over the water and turning the lake into a never-ending expanse of shimmering light.

Brook walked alongside Theo, their strides attuned to the rhythmic creaking of the dock beneath them. Arden had managed to secure them an Airbnb for the next couple of weeks, and it couldn't have been more suitable to their needs. Tucked away just a few properties down from the pier, the lake house provided a sense of seclusion without sacrificing convenience. With ease, they could stroll a short distance to access food and drinks.

The bar and grill restaurant also happened to be the establishment where Adam Bouras had escorted a drunken patron to his vehicle last weekend. Such an altercation should be easy enough to verify, which was imperative to the investigation. If there were three months in between kills, one could assume that the unsub spent a good portion of that time monitoring his victims' daily routines. Feigning a drunken stupor was a good way to meet his target.

"Looks like we're not the only ones with a craving for the catch of the day," Theo commented, his voice low and even. The black eyepatch he wore did little to diminish the perceptiveness of his gaze. "How Bit could want a pizza over those mouthwatering entrees we saw online is beyond me."

"You didn't hear about the list? Bit wants to try pizza and burgers in each state," Brook shared as she took notice of the nearby boats. The majority were ski boats and pontoon boats, though she spotted an occasional fishing craft docked against the pier. "Bit wants to rank the food and put the ratings on some online site that he and Zoey follow. By the way, Zoey's name is in no way connected to the Bureau's case into Kuzmich. It took a while to confirm that fact, by the way."

Bit was currently in a relationship with Zoey Collins. The two of them had been seeing each other since last year, although Theo had been concerned the woman had ulterior motives. Given Bit's personal history with a Russian racketeer, Bit had become a person of interest to the agent investigating Kuzmich's criminal organization. The only reason Bit had been left alone was due to Brook's connection with the Bureau, although Theo's concern regarding Zoey's intention had been valid.

"How solid was your source?"

"As solid as it gets," Brook replied in a tone that indicated the subject wasn't up for discussion. The individual who had made such a confirmation could lose his position inside the Bureau if word ever got out that he shared vital information regarding an ongoing investigation. She pointed toward a sign that had been set off to the side. "Looks like we pick up the takeout order at the bar."

The Crestlake Bar & Grill was located at the end of a wooden pier. The sound of gently lapping waves of the lake created an idyllic setting for a waterfront dining experience. The exterior had a rustic nautical-themed décor, including fishing nets and small anchors. The string of lights hung above the outside seating area probably twinkled after dusk, but it was too bright to make out the illumination right now.

Wooden tables with umbrella-shaded chairs had been strategically arranged along the edge of the pier, offering an unobstructed view of the sunset. The stools at the bar were occupied, but there was a section at the end for a customer to pick up a take-out order. A waitress with a tray of food came around the side wall, denoting a kitchen entrance around the corner of the small structure.

"Seems like everyone's trying to drown out their troubles," Theo murmured as he leaned against the wooden counter. He usually dressed in business casual, but since he had driven most of the way from D.C. to Michigan, he had opted for a pair of dark green joggers and a matching dry-fit shirt. "You mentioned driving to the airport with Graham. Where was he off to today?"

"Somalia," Brook replied as she nodded toward the bartender. The man had gestured that he would be with them shortly before taking an order from a couple at the end of the bar. "Graham mentioned that the trip was only going to be a few days, and then he was returning to D.C. to take his mother out to dinner for her birthday next Wednesday."

Brook and Theo had formed a close friendship since meeting on a federal investigation before the inception of S&E Investigations, Inc. She never would have guessed that he would turn out to be her best friend. She had avoided having someone in her life who Jacob could target like those close to her in high school and college. Both Salley Pearson and Cara Jordan had been brutally murdered due to their close proximity to Brook, and that was a guilt she would carry with her to the grave.

"And yes, I was invited," Brook said before Theo could ask his question. From the way his mouth curled at the sides, he obviously found her predicament amusing. "Graham knows that we're working on an active investigation. If this were a cold case, that would be something else entirely."

"No need to get all defensive," Theo ribbed good-naturedly as he reached for the bowl of peanuts that had been set on the counter. "It's not like the two of you have been together for the past two years."

"Nineteen months is not two years." Brook compressed her lips in agitation when Theo merely smiled his response once again. "Fine. I'm splitting hairs, but I'll have you know that I had to stop by his estate to pick up two of my favorite business suits for this trip. That should count for something."

Theo popped a peanut in his mouth.

"I bought Elizabeth a present, and I made sure to leave it on the table in the foyer." Brook wouldn't have shared any of this information with anyone else. She was left asking herself why she had brought it up in the first place. She loathed being on the defensive. "How is Mia doing?"

Theo laughed as he shook his head.

"You don't get to change the subject. That's not how it works."

"It can work that way if I want it to work that way," Brook muttered, glancing toward the bartender. He didn't seem to be in any hurry to make his way over. "Our food better not be cold."

"In all seriousness, you should fly back on Wednesday to join them for dinner. You would have done so anyway for the class you teach at the college," Theo pointed out before he plucked another peanut from the bowl while giving her a sideways glance. "Finals were yesterday, and now you have one less responsibility to worry about. You have a team for a reason, Brook. Let us do our jobs."

Brook's reason for not wanting to join Graham and his mother for dinner had nothing to do with her lack of faith in the team's ability. She had handpicked them for a reason. She didn't doubt their talents when it came to solving cases as complicated as this one.

Her reasons were personal, and Theo was mindful of that fact.

He understood that Elizabeth Elliott fit the criteria of Jacob's victims. The woman lived what some would call the perfect life, and Brook didn't want to be the reason it was cut short.

"You being at that dinner isn't a catalyst," Theo pointed out as he studied Brook. "The motivation for Jacob has been there for a while, and you separating yourself from the situation doesn't change the facts."

"I blame your father, you know," Brook muttered as she reached for the bowl of peanuts. "There is no one better at giving speeches than a police commissioner."

Theo was prevented from responding when the bartender finally made his way over to them. She still grappled with normalcy after spending a lifetime chasing the horrors of her childhood, though her therapist would convey that she had made great strides to take her life back. Dr. Swift certainly wouldn't be too pleased with how relieved she was to be in Michigan instead of D.C. at the moment.

"Picking up an order?"

"Neville," Theo said, giving his surname the order had been placed under around thirty minutes ago. "Would you throw in some extra tartar sauce?"

"Sure thing." The bartender swiped the receipt from the counter. He then rattled off the order to double-check the entrees. "Looks like you paid over the phone. Give me a second, and I'll grab your order."

"Do you mind if we ask you a few questions first?" Brook had already pulled her credentials from the side pocket of her blazer. She unfolded the black leather billfold and made sure he could clearly visualize the contents. "We're with S&E Investigations, working as consultants with the FBI. There was an altercation that resulted in an inebriated patron being escorted to his vehicle last weekend. You wouldn't happen to know the individuals involved or have security footage of said incident, would you?"

While it was true the owner of the establishment had the right to request a subpoena for such evidence, the owner or manager could also hand over the footage of their own volition. There was no harm in asking for such a favor. While Bit could have easily accessed the footage through unlawful means, the two of them had an unspoken pact to only do so under extreme circumstances. Even then, she trusted him not to leave behind any evidence of such transgression.

"You'll want to speak with Jason Bracco." The bartender's attention shifted when a woman at the end of the bar called out his name. Chip raised a hand that he would be with her in a moment. His interest in the conversation was evident, and it was obvious that he wanted to hear more about why consultants with the FBI were interested in the bar's clientele. "Jason only works the weekend, though. You can find him here tomorrow night. As for security cameras, I'm sorry to tell you that you're out of luck. This place is seasonal, and the owners never bothered to install a system."

"You weren't here last weekend?"

"Oh, I was working alright," Chip replied wryly after reaching behind him for two large white paper bags. He set them on the counter in front of Brook and Theo. "Not a lot of people prefer seasonal work, so it's hard to get reliable bartenders. But the incident you're talking about happened on a Saturday night. This place is crowded on the weekdays, but the weekends are even worse. All I saw was Jason trying to reason with a guy who had too much to drink. Jason and a couple of other customers helped the guy to the parking lot."

"You let the guy drive home?" Theo asked as he didn't bother to hide his skepticism. "Drunk?"

"No, no, it wasn't like that. There are always a couple of drivers parked in the lot. They do a reliable business here. I'm confident that Jason took the guy's keys and handed them to a driver," Chip replied, clearly not wanting to get one of the other employees in trouble with the law. "This might be a tourist spot, but it's still a small town. People take care of their own around here."

"So the man who Jason helped to the parking lot was a regular?"

"I didn't recognize him," Chip said with a slight shrug before taking two Styrofoam cups off a stack next to a fountain machine. He pulled the red and white lever. "Like I said, you'll want to talk to Jason. Wish I could have been more help. Is there something going on that we should know about?"

It wasn't like Chip would be kept in the dark for long about why a private investigative firm had rented out a lake house. Still, Brook was always leery of giving out too much information. She monitored his movements as he began to fill the other cup with Barq's root beer.

"We'll be back tomorrow to speak with Mr. Bracco." Theo pulled a ten-dollar bill from his pocket and stuffed it in the tip jar. He then grabbed both bags off the counter. Chip made sure the to-go cups were secure before sliding the cardboard cupholder across the hard surface. Brook snatched two straws from the container prior to picking up the drinks. "Have a good night."

It was impossible to miss Chip's smile at the hefty-size tip. A lot of customers didn't tip when picking up takeout orders, but there could be a chance that they would need more information in the immediate future. Mary Jane Reynolds had mentioned

Crestlake Bar & Grill as one of her regular weekend hangouts, and there was no better place to sit back and observe one's next victim.

"Depending on where one sits on the back deck of our rental, I bet we have a clear view of the pier," Brook murmured as she fell into step beside Theo. Her black platform pumps were louder against the wooden planks than Theo's running shoes. "It's a public place."

"I'll set up some cameras tonight." Theo nodded toward a couple passing them. "Do you believe the unsub will try to make contact with Mary Jane Reynolds a second time?"

"We don't know that the unsub made contact at all," Brook pointed out as they continued to walk toward the parking lot. There was a small trail that led to the rentals around the lake. "The confrontation with the male subject last weekend was odd enough that it stood out in Mary Jane Reynolds' mind. We can't ignore the run-in, but it stands to reason that the unsub uses the months in between his kills to monitor his victims' routines. If Mary Jane Reynolds decides to frequent this particular establishment in the coming weeks, we're in the perfect place to monitor those in attendance."

"Are you thinking of bringing in outside help?" Theo asked as they stepped off the pier. The path was wide enough that both of them could walk side by side. "You mentioned that the local police assigned an additional patrol car to the area, but is that enough of a security measure?"

"Mary Jane's sister is staying with her for the time being," Brook said as she lifted her face to the evening breeze.

The delicious aromas of the bar and grill hung heavy in the air, and Brook hadn't had a chance to eat during the day. Once she had some sustenance, she would use the rest of the evening hours to dive into the profile.

"If the time comes that we feel Mary Jane Reynolds from Crestlake, Michigan is the unsub's next target, we'll make sure a team is in place. In the meantime, once you have the name and photograph of the inebriated male subject who bothered Mary Jane last weekend, I'm going to need you to make the two-hour drive to Mount Pleasant. We need to re-question the families and friends of the previous victims. With any luck, you'll find something to tie all three cases together before the unsub can claim his next victim."

CHAPTER FIVE

Sylvie Deering

May 2024

Thursday — 10:02 pm

THE FULL MOON GLIMMERED in the night sky, hanging low and heavy over the serene lake. The reflection danced on the water's surface while a cool breeze rustled through the trees. It was as if nature had paused and taken a deep breath, which was the exact peaceful ambiance that Sylvie had needed this evening. She relished the sound of crickets and the flashing lights of the lightning bugs.

Life was a beautiful thing.

Sylvie reached for the hot cup of tea that she had made before settling comfortably in one of the loungers on the back deck of the rental house. She had dimmed the glowing screen to make it easier to read the pages of text that hopefully held some answers to the list of questions regarding the case. She lightly blew on the surface of her favorite beverage while scanning the statements taken from family members and friends of the victims.

The testimonies taken had detailed the lives cut brutally short, but nothing in the depictions gave any indication that someone new might have entered the lives of the deceased. Brook's initial profile suggested that the unsub monitored his victims for months. If the unsub hadn't inserted himself into their lives, someone should have noticed a stranger keeping such close tabs on these particular women.

The soft shush of the sliding glass door cut through the numerous conversations of the crickets. They didn't seem bothered by the noise, either.

Bit stepped over the threshold with a throw blanket in his hand. His grey knitted hat, crafted by his sister, covered most of his blonde hair. He recently had a trim, but the strands still hung well below his ears. She pushed her glasses up the bridge of her nose so that he couldn't miss the judgment in her eyes.

"I'm fine, Bit."

It wasn't that she didn't appreciate the team's concern for her well-being. They were family to her, and she would have acted in the same manner had one of them been stabbed three times in the abdomen. She didn't deny that the attack had been brutal and life-changing, but every time one of them treated her differently was a reminder that she had let her guard down.

"It's getting cold out here," Bit said as he closed the distance between them. He stood there awkwardly but also in an endearing sort of way. "I would have done the same for Boss. Here. Take the blanket."

Sylvie hid a smile as she rested her teacup on the wooden arm of the lounger. She lifted her laptop so that Bit could cover her legs with the blanket. Instantly, the thick material chased away the chill of the night.

"Thank you," Sylvie murmured in appreciation as she resettled the laptop on her thighs. "Anything back on the birth certificates of Mary Two and Three?"

"Not yet, but we should have them within the hour." Bit shifted his stance, which was a telltale sign that he had more to say on the previous topic. "Maybe it's not about you."

"I know," Sylvie responded sincerely as she glanced behind him toward the sliding glass door. Theo was at the kitchen table, though Brook was nowhere to be found. She was probably in the living room fleshing out the profile. "Part of me is glad that it wasn't the other way around."

Sylvie had heard from Arden the truth about her time in the hospital. She had been in the ICU for a while after a cardiac episode while her father had been at home dying from pancreatic cancer. She had thought she had a handle on things preparing for his care, and she had resolutely pushed aside the offers of help. Had she not done so, she wouldn't have missed the fact that the health aide assigned by the agency to take care of her father wasn't in fact the same woman hired by said agency.

Jacob Matthew Walsh had penetrated their lives through someone else, and now there was no denying his reach. He had the ability to truly hurt them, and the taste of death had afforded Sylvie a better understanding of why Brook had closed herself off over the years. Sylvie was in awe of the courage Brook had shown by letting down her emotional barriers.

"It wasn't all bad," Bit said as he attempted to lighten the mood in his usual manner. He didn't do well with serious conversations. "The hospital had great chocolate pudding."

"You also kept stealing my JELL-O cups," Sylvie replied as she reached for her teacup. "Speaking of food, did you save me a slice of pizza?"

"Two slices." Bit took a seat in one of the four chairs next to her that belonged to a large round table. "I've ranked the pizza seven out of the twelve states we've either stayed at or driven through. Tomorrow, I'll order the bacon cheeseburger with fries."

"Only seven out of twelve?" Sylvie scrunched her nose in disappointment. The crust had been coated with what appeared to be a delicious buttery parmesan mixture. "That's disappointing."

"Not as disappointed as Zoey's parents are going to be when they meet me," Bit said as he adjusted his knit hat. He was also jostling his leg to the point that her tea was sloshing against the rim. She quickly took a large enough sip so that she wouldn't spill any liquid on her laptop. "I don't do parents."

"No one does parents," Sylvie responded with a laugh. "Bit, they will love you because you make their daughter happy. I'm sure that is all they care about."

Bit and Sylvie had carefully navigated their relationship since they both came to work for S&E Investigations. Quite simply, he was her best friend. They were so close that the lines had blurred, and they had even entertained the trajectory of something more intimate. She loved him...but as a friend who knew her battle scars and still chose to love her back. She cherished the balance they had struck, and he was a consistent presence who never asked for more than she could give.

It was clear that Zoey made Bit happy. After nearly losing her own life just three months ago, Sylvie fully grasped just how precious and rare such happiness could be in the grand scheme of things.

"Zoey said the same thing, but did you know that her father is a highly renowned orthopedic?" Bit asked as he subconsciously studied Theo's handiwork on the security camera aimed at the Crestlake Bar & Grill. Sylvie figured it wouldn't be long before Bit was adjusting the angle. "That means the family has money, and I was under the impression that Zoey didn't care about material things. Don't get me wrong. I have more money now than I know what to do with, but—"

"That is so not true." Sylvie was mindful not to spill her tea. She took another sip before finishing her side of the discussion. "You own practically every tech gadget ever made. You even bought that robot dog that can fetch your energy drinks from the kitchen."

"Hey, that was a good investment," Bit defended as he finally stood up to get a closer look at the hardware of the security camera. "Speaking of robots, this case reminds me of that movie."

"What movie?"

"You know the one," Bit said as he reached into the right pocket of his jeans. Within seconds, he had his Swiss Army knife opened to adjust one of the screws. "Where a robot is sent back from the future to kill a woman who is destined to be the mother of the man who is the leader of the resistance. The robot takes on a human form, and he only knows the woman's name...not what she looks like. So he starts killing all the women with the same name. Excellent movie, but my point is that this case reminds me of that plot."

Sylvie credited the caffeine from the black tea leaves for her ability to follow along with such an intricate storyline. She took another sip just in case.

"Bit, I'm relatively certain that I can guarantee robots weren't sent from the future to kill off all the Mary Jane Reynolds who reside in the state of Michigan," Sylvie replied wryly as she finally set down her teacup. "I've been scrolling through the statements taken by the local police, focusing on family members of the deceased and close friends of the victims. No one made any claim that there was someone new in their lives. Would you check to see if there were any 911 calls near the victims' residences? Look for any calls about suspicious persons in those areas, including break-ins."

"Sure," Bit said as he nodded more to himself than her over correcting the angle of the security camera to his specifications. He retreated a few steps as he folded his Swiss Army knife to store it back in his pocket. "I can also do the same for—"

The sound of the sliding glass door being opened drew both Sylvie and Bit's attention. Theo leaned out, keeping ahold of the handle.

"Mary Two and Three—they weren't adopted," Theo disclosed in disappointment. "We're back to square one, at least until Brook finishes her profile."

Sylvie sighed in frustration, but she had no doubt that they would find a dangling thread at some point. As a former federal analyst, she had never been out in the field before taking a position with S&E Investigations. Working with Theo had given her insight on what to look for during interviews, and studying Brook's preferred method had afforded Sylvie the ability to understand the importance of profiling. Arden was old school, and Bit's expertise wasn't something that could easily be learned even if one was by his side twenty-four-seven.

Sylvie closed her laptop with a soft click and set it on the chair that Bit had vacated moments before. The night had grown colder, and Bit had been wise to bring her a blanket. She shouldn't have let pride control her response to the kind gesture. What she needed right now was another cup of tea before settling in the living room.

"Big T, have you ever watched the movie where a robot is sent back from the future and..."

Sylvie couldn't help but smile as she stood from the lounger. Bit always made her day brighter. She took her time to hang the blanket over her arm before collecting her laptop, phone, and half-empty teacup, thinking over the lack of information they had to sort through.

The team had their work cut out for them.

The Bureau had reached out to Brook a couple of hours ago and politely requested she put together a press release. They were basically covering their asses, demanding that S&E Investigations convey the importance that anyone with the name Mary Jane Reynolds living in the state of Michigan should keep a close eye on her surroundings. Should anything stand out, they were to contact their local police. The FBI had also stressed to Brook that the press release wasn't meant to cause panic, leaving her in a very precarious situation.

With Theo driving to Mount Pleasant in the next couple of days, that still left two crime scenes that hadn't been walked through by someone on the team. Granted, those locations had been released to the families of the victims, but it would still be beneficial to the investigation to get a firsthand examination.

Local police reports sometimes left out details that came into play later, and those detectives hadn't known to look for any connections to other crimes. Given that Lansing was only an hour and a half away from Crestlake, it was less time than it would take Theo to drive to Mount Pleasant.

Sylvie understood that the others were concerned for her health, but she had been cleared for fieldwork by her physician. An expert's opinion held more weight than the concern of friends, and she meant that in the nicest way possible. Maybe, just maybe, taking some time to get her feet back underneath her was exactly what she needed for some normalcy.

CHAPTER SIX

Theo Neville

May 2024

Friday — 5:21 pm

THE PATRONS OF CRESTLAKE Bar & Grill were reveling in their Friday night freedom after a grueling workweek. Every table, chair, and stool was occupied by individuals eager to unwind and let loose. The air was alive with the sound of laughter, glasses clinking together in celebration, and silverware clanking against plates as delicious food was devoured. The lively chatter and upbeat music from the live band drowned out the usual peaceful existence surrounding the lake.

As Theo closed the distance to the bar, his presence was observed by the bartender. Chip lifted a hand and gestured toward the side entrance. Theo nodded his appreciation before advancing in that direction. He didn't have to walk far, though. A young man clutching an empty gray container emerged from around the corner toward what had to be the only empty table on the pier.

"Jason Bracco?" Theo had made sure to hold up his credentials. He didn't react at all when Jason's gaze was drawn to the black eyepatch. "I'm Theo Neville, and I work for a private investigative firm. We're consulting with the FBI on an active investigation. I'd like to ask you a few questions regarding an altercation that happened here last weekend."

"You're talking about Mary Jane," Jason said with a nod of understanding. His gaze drifted toward a table. Theo had already been made aware that Mary Jane and her sister had planned an evening out with their friends. The media presence had died off, and she was now going about her daily routine with a lot more followers. Brook spoke to Mary Jane this afternoon on the phone to clarify some information. "After that video she posted the other day, that's all anyone can talk about. Are you thinking the drunk guy that hit on her killed those other women?"

"We're just gathering information," Theo explained, purposefully keeping his response vague. He slipped his credentials back into the pocket of his khakis. "Would you walk me through what happened last weekend?"

"A guy got a little handsy with some of the ladies, and a few of the other customers escorted him to the parking lot. I helped, but only to make sure that the guy didn't get into his car," Jason explained as he continued to load the dirty dishes into the gray container. "The owners have a strict policy about not allowing our patrons to drink and drive if we believe they've had one too many."

"I take it that Mary Jane Reynolds is a regular here?" Theo asked, wanting a little more background. "What about her fiancé?"

"Mary Jane is usually here with her sister and friends. Usually on a Saturday night. There is a local bar in town that a lot of people go to on Friday evenings." Jason reached for the empty glasses. "As for Adam, not so much. I think he travels a lot for his job."

"It sounds like you know them pretty well," Theo observed as he shifted his stance so that he had a better view of the patrons. No one seemed particularly interested in Mary Jane's table. "Are you a local?"

"Born and raised," Jason said, though not with pride. "Went to college, got a job in Lansing, and then was laid off six months later. I had no choice but to move back home."

"It's not easy out there," Theo said in commiseration before steering the conversation back to the topic at hand. "What about the man you helped escort to the parking lot? Is he a local?"

"No," Jason said with a shake of his head. He took the wet rag that had been hanging over the side of the gray bucket and began to wipe down the table. "Vacationer. He kept complaining about the drivers between here and Mount Pleasant. Made it sound like he had dodged bullets rather than slow cars on his way to Crestlake. He was a bit dramatic, but it was probably the alcohol talking. Hunter might know more."

"Hunter?"

"Hunter Darrisaw. He and Mindy served the tables last Saturday night." Jason motioned toward a young woman setting two plates of food down in front of a couple. "Hunter has the night off, though. He got tickets to the comedy club in town."

Theo made a mental note to speak with Hunter at a later date. "Was the intoxicated patron by himself?"

"Yeah." Jason tossed the rag on top of the dirty dishes, but he made no move to pick up the gray bucket. "Come to think of it, I found it odd that he chose to sit at one of the tables instead of the bar."

"Do you know if Mary Jane was already seated at her table? Or did she and her party arrive afterward?"

"I couldn't tell you, man."

"Did the guy pay for his drinks with cash or card?"

"I'm not sure." A crease formed between Jason's brows as he clearly fought for a memory that was within countless of interactions that he had on a daily basis. "Actually, I'm not sure. You would have to check with Hunter or Chip. Mindy was working last weekend, but I don't think the guy sat in her section. You can ask her, though."

"Thanks, Jason." Theo reached into his other pocket to collect one of his business cards. He extended his hand, offering Jason his contact information. "If you think of anything else that sticks out to you, give me a call. Also, if the guy comes back here, I'd really appreciate it if you gave me a heads-up."

"No problem," Jason said as he took the card. He glanced at the information before tucking the card into the pocket of his jeans underneath his waist apron. "I hope you find out who murdered those women."

After Jason picked up the dirty dishes and disappeared around the corner, Theo turned toward the bar. The thumping bass from the speakers in front of the live band pulsated through the wooden planks beneath his feet. All the stools were taken, so Theo leaned against the end of the counter while waiting for a chance to speak with the waitress. He would have asked Chip about the payment from last Saturday, but the bartender was busy pouring drinks and exchanging banter with those at the bar. The opportunity to speak with Mindy finally came when she walked up to the bar.

"Do you have a takeout order?" Mindy asked as she set her tray on top of the bar. "We're slammed tonight, but I can help you."

"How many servers usually work on a Thursday night?"

"Three," Mindy replied before walking around to the side entrance. It wasn't long before she appeared with two bags of food and a drink carrier. "Neville, right?"

"That's right," Theo said as he checked the number of containers inside the bags. Once he was confident that their entire order had been included, he reached into his back pocket and pulled out his wallet. He shoved another ten-dollar bill into the tip jar. "Theo Neville. A colleague and I were here yesterday, talking to Chip about the altercation that happened last weekend. My firm is consulting with the FBI on an investigation, and Jason said that you might have waited on the guy who was escorted to the parking lot."

"Hard to forget the asshole who put his hand on my ass," Mindy muttered in disgust. "He hasn't been back, either. I didn't serve him, though. Hunter had that privilege."

"Do you happen to know if the guy paid by credit card or cash? We're looking for a name."

"Why?" Mindy asked as she made no move to exit the bar area. As a matter of fact, she leaned her forearms against the counter with interest. "Did he rob a bank or something?"

"You didn't see Mary Jane's video, did you?" Chip asked as he set two cocktails on Mindy's tray. "The Feds are investigating those murders that are connected, and these guys are helping out."

"I've been in class all week," Mindy complained as she turned to Chip. "What murders?"

"There were three women living in Michigan, all named Mary Jane Reynolds. They were stabbed to death. The Mary Jane who lives in Crestlake posted a video about it, and she gained enough attention that the Feds have taken over the murder investigations."

Theo remained silent, allowing Chip to fill Mindy in on all the details. Oftentimes, personal conversations let things slip that could be beneficial to a case. Unfortunately, the only piece of information that Theo had picked up on was that Mindy was a college student with a busy schedule.

"And you think that the guy who put his hand on my ass could have killed those women?" Mindy asked in disbelief, turning her attention back to Theo.

"I didn't say that," Theo assured her. "I'm merely trying to find out if he paid by cash or credit card."

"Credit card. I saw him hand the card to Hunter, because right afterward, the guy noticed the group of women sitting at the table next to his."

Theo hid his frustration. A warrant would need to be granted to get his hands on those receipts. While Mindy offered up more information, Theo unclipped his phone from the case attached to his belt. He constructed a quick email with the information and sent it to Sylvie.

"You wouldn't happen to have those receipts here, would you?" There was no harm in asking if the employees would give up the receipts voluntarily. "Or, by chance, remember the man's name?"

"I'm pretty sure Randy takes home all the money and receipts on a nightly basis," Mindy replied as she flashed a smile toward Chip when he set a draft beer down on the tray next to the two cocktail drinks. "Randy and his brother, Todd, own the place. They come by around eleven o'clock every night to cash out. As for remembering the guy's name, I think it might have been Dave or Dan. Maybe Dale. I just remember his name starting with D."

Theo's phone vibrated against his thigh. Mindy left her position behind the bar, but she eventually came around to collect the drinks.

"You've been extremely helpful, Mindy. Thank you."

"I hope you catch the guy."

Theo waited until Mindy had walked away before checking his phone. Sylvie had replied to his text that Bit had located the driver who had taken a passenger by the name of Daniel Callaghan to a lake house located twenty minutes away.

No warrant was needed, and Sylvie had already put in for a background check. Once the report came in, Brook would almost certainly pay the man a visit first thing in the morning.

Theo carried the two takeout bags in one hand while holding the cup holder in the other. He scanned every table and patron on his way out, not noticing anyone out of place. No male subject seemed to be alone, and no one appeared to be focused on Mary Jane Reynold's table. Theo wasn't concerned that he would miss anything since Bit was keeping close tabs on the security footage gathered by the camera pointed toward the pier.

Whether or not Daniel Callaghan turned up any red flags, Theo would be taking a two-hour drive to Mount Pleasant tomorrow morning after dropping Sylvie off at a rental car center. She was adamant that she be the one to personally interview the family of Mary Two.

"Excuse me."

Theo had just stepped off the pier and onto the path that led in the direction of the lake house. An older woman maybe in her late fifties stood in front of him with her phone in hand. On the display was a picture of Brook and Theo from an old article posted online during a previous case.

"You're Theo Neville, aren't you? From S&E Investigations?"

"Yes, ma'am," Theo replied cautiously as he glanced around the parking lot. He spotted a man standing near a vehicle with a Michigan license plate. It was obvious that the man had accompanied the woman to the restaurant. "How may I help you?"

"We saw on Mary Jane Reynold's social media that she would be at the Crestlake Bar & Grill this evening, so we took the chance that someone from your firm would be here, as well," the woman replied before glancing over her shoulder. She looked vaguely familiar. "That's my husband."

Once she was satisfied that her spouse was nearby, the woman turned her attention back to Theo. He wasn't thrilled that Mary Jane was posting her locations on social media. Such foolish action could end up getting her killed, which meant that someone from the team would need to have a conversation with her sooner rather than later.

"What can I do for you, Mrs..."

"Reynolds. Mary Jane Reynolds," she replied as tears filled her eyes. Theo realized immediately that he was speaking with the Mary Jane who resided in the northern part of the state. She must have cut her hair recently, because the photograph on file depicted her with long hair. "My husband and I are from Petosky, and I think someone has been following me for the past week. I'm frightened, Mr. Neville. I think I'm the killer's next target."

CHAPTER SEVEN

Brooklyn Sloane

May 2024

Saturday — 6:29 am

"I WAS ABLE TO convince the Reynolds to drive back home later today, but only because we gave our word that she would have round-the-clock protection. We'll need to do the same with the other women bearing the same name throughout Michigan."

Brook's lungs burned with the brisk, morning air as she and Theo crested the small incline from the pier to the lake house. The steady rhythm of their running shoes thudded against the hard cement of the sidewalk. Gradually, they slowed to a walk until they came to a stop to begin their stretching regimen. Her favorite exercise was balancing on one foot while bringing the heel of her other shoe against her backside.

The relief in her thigh was palpable.

The bright sun had crested the horizon maybe fifteen minutes ago, and neither she nor Theo had spoken a word since they had left the house...until now. Their moment of peace had come to an end.

They had gotten into a morning routine when on field assignments, and she never would have expected that having company on a morning run could be so enjoyable. There was comfort in unity.

Brook wiped a bead of sweat from her brow, her pulse still echoing in her ears even though her heart rate had steadily slowed while she finished her stretches. Her thigh hadn't twinged once during her morning jog, and she was very pleased with the healing process.

"I've placed a few calls, and I'm confident that we'll get approval for the additional safety measures. Although you're right, and most will probably be at a local level."

Theo led the way to the front door of the rental house. They crossed the threshold into the coolness of the living room. The delicious aroma of coffee filled the air, but that was only because Brook had preset the coffee maker to brew a full pot by the time they arrived back from their run. She would have a glass of water first, but there was nothing like that first sip of coffee in the morning.

Bit was sitting at a makeshift desk in the middle of the room. He lifted a hand in greeting without interrupting his focus, obviously not completely lost in whatever was happening on the screen in front of him. His head was bouncing with the beat of his music streaming out of his headphones while the numerous monitors on the long, rectangular table flickered with activity. He was running a multitude of programs with information about their victims to find a common thread. She was confident that he would eventually be successful in that endeavor.

"Donuts," Brook announced in victory, pointing toward the half-eaten jelly donut on a plate next to Bit's energy drink. "I hope he picked out some chocolate ones."

"I don't know how you can eat a donut right after a run," Theo muttered good-naturedly as he moved through the living room toward the kitchen. "I need a good hour before I can digest anything other than my protein shake."

Brook admired Theo's 'everything in moderation' outlook. Sylvie had recently taken on a healthier lifestyle with great success due to monitoring Theo's daily regimen.

"I will have you know that a donut covered with chocolate icing hits three of the five food groups," Brook informed him as she followed behind, pausing only to pick up her tablet that she had left on the side table. "And don't you dare say that I'm rationalizing when I haven't had my coffee yet."

The interior of the lake house was an eclectic mix of modernism anchored in rustic charm. Exposed wooden beams traversed the ceiling, while sleek, metal light fixtures dangled above. Their dim light cast soft pools of illumination over the hardwood floors. While there was a hearth surrounded by river rock on the far wall, it was currently too warm for a fire. Instead, Bit had positioned the large 4k portable screen that served as their murder board in front of the fireplace.

Theo crossed into the kitchen first, which was in contrast to the dim makeshift operations center that they had set up in the living room. The bright morning light bounced off the lake's surface, filtering through the sliding glass door and the wide window above the sink. Sunrays generated a shimmering dance across the white marble countertops and stainless steel appliances.

Brook walked over to the sliding glass door, pulling on the handle until the door stood slightly ajar. An inviting, cool breeze brushed over her face, and she inhaled the faintest hint of pine and freshwater.

No fragrance could cut through the aroma of coffee, though.

Theo was already holding out a glass of water by the time she turned around. She took the proffered drink before monitoring his progress to the fridge. Along the way, he swiped a napkin from the counter to wipe away the perspiration from his brow, taking extra care around his eye patch.

He retrieved his protein shake before letting the fridge door close on its own. The cap gave way with one simple twist, and he leaned against the counter to take a long, replenishing drink.

"You haven't mentioned Mia in a while," Brook said after she had polished off her water. She then set the glass gently in the sink. "Everything okay between the two of you?"

Jacob's previous actions of having someone infiltrate their lives in such an intimate manner had affected every one of them. Sylvie's decision to go with a home health agency should not have resulted in a woman stealing another woman's identity, inserting herself into Sylvie's life to learn every profound detail, before then attempting to take Sylvie's life. Bit was the only one who seemed to be able to strengthen his relationship with Zoey, while the rest of them had been left to put up additional barriers.

"I asked Mia to join us at the pub on our next Thursday night outing, whenever that might be," Theo said, his smile breaking free after he lowered his protein shake. Apparently, Bit wasn't the only one who had been able to move on. Brook was always astonished with how time could heal some wounds. She reached for the coffee cup that she had set out next to the coffee maker. "You'll like her."

"I have no doubt," Brook said, meaning every word as she continued to pour the contents of the carafe into her cup. Sometimes, she wished she could just insert a straw into the machine. "From what you told me about Mia, she understands our work and respects your time. That's a rare combination to have in a relationship."

Her fingers wrapped around the mug before leaning back against the counter so that she could face Theo. The welcoming steam curled upwards, and she couldn't help but inhale deeply before taking her first sip. As she lowered her cup, her gaze landed on a colorful box with its lid open on the countertop of the island. The jelly donut that Bit had already confiscated had left behind a noticeable void among its pastry companions. Fortunately, she spotted two chocolate donuts on the lefthand side of the box.

"You have it with Graham," Theo pointed out as he lifted his bottle once more.

"I do," Brook agreed softly as she couldn't suppress her own smile. "But Graham's entire career was spent in the military. He understands the demands of the job."

It was rare that Graham was able to call during his trips, but he had managed to call her via video last night. They had spent a good hour talking about their views on what constituted incredible modern art. It was silly, but she had appreciated the distraction.

"Have you decided if you're flying back to D.C. on Wednesday to have dinner with his mother?" Theo asked, causing her hand to pause mid-air, her cup inches from her lips. Fortunately, Sylvie's sudden presence prevented Brook from having to reply. "Don't think that lets you off the hook."

Brook feigned ignorance before turning her attention to Sylvie.

"Morning," Brook said as she took in Sylvie's appearance. She had dressed comfortably for the upcoming trip to Lansing, but she had also maintained an air of professionalism with the soft pink blouse that she had paired with white denim. Her pink pumps matched, as well as her earrings. Brook was happy to observe Sylvie's vigor to dive into work. "All set for the drive out to Lansing?"

"I contacted Mary Two's husband, and he's meeting me at his residence later this morning." Sylvie's blue eyes lit up at the sight of donuts. She immediately reached for a napkin and didn't speak again until she had taken a bite out of a blueberry cake donut. Her eyes rolled in satisfaction. "This is delicious. And I don't want to hear one word out of you, Theo. Everything in moderation, right? And on another note, Bit should start a rating system for bakeries."

"Moderation is key," Theo said in agreement before switching the conversation back to the case. "It's hard to believe that Mary Two's husband didn't sell the house. They have a daughter. You'd think that he would want a fresh start."

"Well, his daughter might be the reason that he hasn't sold the house," Sylvie pointed out after licking the corner of her lip. "Their daughter has already been through so much, maybe it's best to keep her in the same routine."

Brook snapped her fingers, causing both Theo and Sylvie to glance her way. The fact that Mary Two hadn't been born Mary Jane Reynolds had special meaning, and it was imperative she cover the profile thus far before Theo and Sylvie headed out for the day.

"Let's gather in the living room to go over the profile." Brook pushed off the counter. She made sure to top off her coffee, tuck her tablet underneath her arm, and snatch a chocolate donut from the box before proceeding toward the small hallway. "There are a few things you should know before interviewing the family members and friends."

"I'll be in shortly," Sylvie said as she set her donut on the napkin. "I'm going to make a cup of tea."

Theo remained behind with Sylvie while Brook walked into the living room. Bit was still in his zone, head bobbing to the beat of his music. He reached up and pulled his headphones off when he caught sight of her.

"Hey, Boss. I can confirm that the first three victims had no contact with each other online. As far as the data goes, they did not know one another."

"Thanks, Bit." Brook carefully set her items down on a side table, keeping ahold of her coffee. She would have preferred to have taken a shower before their meeting, but she understood

Sylvie's desire to get a start on her day. "Would you please add Arden to the meeting?"

With a few keystrokes, Bit was able to connect with Arden in their D.C. offices. While it was a Saturday and quite early in the morning, Arden had assured them that he would be available to join in on any meetings regarding the investigation.

"Good morning," Arden greeted with his usual morning smile. His mustache was more salt than pepper, and he had deep laugh lines etched into his weathered features. Brook was able to detect from his background that he wasn't sitting at his desk, but rather in the large conference room. Doing so gave him the ability to view the same information on the large 4k monitor as the one Bit had brought with them to Michigan. "How is the rental? I made sure the living room was large enough to accommodate all the equipment."

"The house is perfect, Arden," Brook responded as she stood in front of the portable monitor. "Were you able to do the same in Ann Arbor, just in case we need to change locations?"

"Yes, and I also took the liberty of doing the same in Mount Pleasant and Lansing." Arden's gaze drifted over Brook's shoulder. It was evident that he wanted to know who else was within earshot, but she quickly shook her head to dispel any attempt at discussing the kitten. He understood and kept the conversation casual. "I only needed to put small deposits on the other Airbnb locations. The owners understood our situation, and they were very accommodating."

"Morning, Arden," Theo greeted as he entered the living room. He must have polished off his protein shake. A bottle of water was in his hand, though he hadn't removed the cap yet. "How goes the battle?"

"Depends on which battle you speak of," Arden said with a hearty laugh. "According to the eye doctor, I'll need cataract surgery soon."

"What's this about surgery?" Sylvie asked with concern as she joined them. She usually preferred to boil her water in a kettle, but she must have slipped a cup of water into the microwave for her tea. She came to a stop beside Brook with a teacup in hand. "Can it wait until we're back? I'd like to be there, Arden."

"Oh, you don't have to—"

"Gumshoe, you know that you can't win an argument against Little T," Bit warned as he righted his knitted cap after knocking it askew with his headphones. "How do they numb your eyes? Drops? Needles? I heard this story about—"

"The unsub," Brook stated loudly in an effort to avert Bit from upsetting Arden with stories of surgeries gone wrong. Brook closed the distance to the portable monitor. Since it was a touch screen, she was able to move the video of Arden to the side. His shoulders were shaking from laughing at Bit, who still didn't seem to understand where he had gone wrong with his questions. "Caucasian male, mid-twenties to mid-thirties. Even if we were working without the autopsy reports, which do happen to indicate the force at which the victims were stabbed with a fixed-blade knife, the profile points toward a male subject. DNA from the first two crime scenes is a match, but the unsub is not in the system. We're still waiting on the forensics report from the Mount Pleasant crime scene. This isn't your textbook serial killer, though. Something very specific drives him. I do not believe that he kills for the sake of killing or satisfying some sexual fantasy. The unsub is charming, sociable, and blends in seamlessly with his surroundings."

"Profession?"

The inquiry had come from Sylvie, who had taken a seat on the couch. She set her tea on the side table while finishing off what was left of her blueberry donut.

"White collar," Brook replied as she pulled her profile up on the screen. As usual, she had made bullet points for easy reference. "The killer most likely has the ability to work remotely.

The combination affords him the time needed to study the daily routines of his victims."

"After last night, the killer has two potential victims in Crestlake," Theo pointed out grimly as he pulled a seat out from underneath the table. Bit reached for his donut and energy drink to move them to the other side of his workstation. "By the way, I listed the wife of the couple last night as Mary Five into the software program."

Brook had spent a good portion of the evening on the phone last night with Agent Tirelli. He had agreed it was in the Bureau's best interest to give every Mary Jane Reynolds in the state of Michigan some type of protection, whether through their local law enforcement or a federal agent. Tirelli had also agreed to make the arrangements. He would have another federal agent contact all Mary Jane Reynolds, with the exception of Mary Five, whom Theo had personally escorted to and stayed with at the hotel until the arrival of a local state trooper.

"The murder of Mary Two points to the motive that the kills are not about women born with the name Mary Jane Reynolds," Brook pointed out after taking a sip of her coffee. She then reached out to the screen and closed down her profile. She opened the three crime scene photos. "I'd like for the two of you to take photos of the crime scene for comparison. Mary Three was the only victim wounded in the back, while the other two were stabbed in the chest. Considering that Mary Three was on her morning run, we can assume that the unsub isn't searching for something specific. Bit, can you conduct a street view of the jogging trail where Mary Three was killed?"

"Sure thing, Boss." Bit glanced up from his screen. "I still haven't found any connections between the victims. One married, one engaged, and one single...the list of differences is endless."

"Could that be it?" Sylvie asked as she crumbled a napkin in her hand. She reached over for her teacup before settling back against the cushion. "The victims' differences?"

"No," Brook murmured, confident in her summation. "If we take out Mary Four, who is thankfully still alive, only one victim was adopted. Two victims were raised in loving households. One victim has a child, the other two do not. I believe there is a connection, and we will find it in due time."

"Before I forget," Arden interjected, garnering everyone's attention. "Theo, a rental car is waiting for you at the car agency. I scheduled you to have it for the next few days, but I can easily extend it if need be."

"I appreciate that, Arden."

"I'll be speaking with Daniel Callaghan today," Brook informed them as she finally stepped away from the monitor. "Bit located the rental house that he booked for the week. His preliminary background check states that he is thirty-two years of age, an electrician, and also happens to be going through a divorce. Bit discovered through Callaghan's social media that he is meeting some old high school friends to fish for the week. Evidently, he arrived a day early. He may not fit our profile, but he could have seen something last weekend when he was fixated on Mary Four. Afterward, I'm going to place a call to the detective who investigated the first murder in Ann Arbor. Depending on what he has to say, I might be taking a drive out there."

"That's a two-and-a-half-hour drive," Arden pointed out with a frown. "I can call one of the private airstrips. Maybe someone can fly you there and back."

"I'll keep you posted on my plans," Brook said before taking a sip of her coffee. "Arden, anything on the home front?"

"We received a call regarding a cold case in Minnesota," Arden replied, his gaze being drawn off-screen. "Four victims between

2016 and 2018. Lit on fire, and left to die. From what I gather, the investigation never made it into the hands of the FBI."

"Email me the information, and I'll reach out to the caller later today." Brook's curiosity was piqued, but she pushed it on the back burner. "To finish, the three victims also had very different professions—teacher, accountant, and sales. Theo and Sylvie, include colleagues in your list of people to interview."

"Sylvie, will you drop me off at the car agency?" Theo asked as he stood from the chair. He had finished his water, and he carried the empty bottle with him toward the kitchen. "Give me ten minutes to shower and dress. I'll—"

A timid meow could be heard through the speaker of the portable monitor, but it was so faint that it could have been mistaken for a figment of one's imagination. Arden immediately began to whine in a high-pitched voice before wincing to finish out the charade. "Ah, damn charley horse. That's my cue to go and eat a banana. Call if you need anything."

No one in the living room said a word as the video feed disappeared from the screen. Bit coughed, Theo rubbed his mouth to prevent Sylvie from catching his smile, and Brook merely continued to sip her coffee. She had warned them that it was a bad idea to pick up the kitten while they were out of the city.

Fortunately, Brook's cell phone rang, creating a diversion. She walked over to the side table where she had left her phone to charge, recognizing the number on the display. The agent in charge of finding Stella Bennett's remains was reaching out to her, which meant a team was about to start their grid search of the area that used to house the cabins for summer camp.

When Jacob had turned himself into the FBI, he had done so with the purpose of luring Sarah Evanston out of WITSEC. She had been the only woman to survive one of his horrific attacks, and he couldn't stand that she had gone into hiding. Betting that she would believe it was safe to live her life once again, Jacob had taken extreme measures to entice her out of safety.

Fortunately, Brook had managed to convince Sarah to remain in the witness protection program, knowing full well that part of the deal to take the death penalty off the table was to give a list of victims' names. Brook's brother never would have given up his freedom without having a backup plan. Several of them, in fact.

Only Jacob had left one name off the list—Stella Bennett.

Should the remains of the young girl be discovered and her death traced back to 1996, it could result in devastating consequences for Jacob. A trial would ensue, and with it...the death penalty.

CHAPTER EIGHT

Brooklyn Sloane

May 2024

Saturday — 10:43 am

A COOL BREEZE MADE its way across the small lake, ruffling the surface of the water. The small house that Daniel Callaghan had rented for the week had been built at an angle, affording any visitors a picturesque scene of a small pier and a fishing boat. The temperature was set to hit the mid-seventies later this afternoon, but a storm front was blowing in from the west. The threat of rain could be the reason why the group of friends had decided not to get in one last day of fishing before their flights home tomorrow.

Brook's black kitten heels crunched against the gravel path as she approached the front of the house. She stepped onto the porch, but there were no railings surrounding the worn wooden planks. Someone had left the inside entrance open to allow fresh air to infiltrate the screened door. She raised her hand and rapped her knuckles on the thin frame.

As Brook waited for either Daniel Callaghan or one of his friends to make an appearance, she replayed her conversation with the federal agent leading the search for Stella Bennett's remains. Special Agent Dever had spoken of new methods, recent technology, and the latest equipment to accomplish the task at hand. She wasn't one to hope, knowing how futile such a gesture could be in the grand scheme of life, but she couldn't deny her impatience to follow through with her promise to ensure Jacob was punished for his crimes.

A promise that she had made to her brother's victims, their families, and herself.

"May I help you?"

The man who greeted her through the screen door was not Daniel Callaghan. His driver's license and social media pictures depicted blue eyes, a rather flat nose, and a square jaw with an unkempt beard. The male subject standing before her had slightly wavy brown hair, matching eyes, and angular features. He also wore a designer watch that probably cost more than Daniel Callaghan's annual salary.

"My name is Brooklyn Sloane." She already had her credentials in hand, so she held up the identification for him to view. He appeared more interested in her sidearm, which had become visible as she held up her hand. "I'm with S&E Investigations, and we are consulting with the FBI on a murder investigation. I was hoping to speak with Daniel Callaghan. Is he here right now?"

By this time, the man had used one hand to open the door and keep it that way for her to enter. She didn't appreciate that he remained in place, making it necessary for her to brush past him with mere inches separating their bodies.

"Dan is upstairs packing for his flight home. I'm a friend of his—Cav Buckley." Cav held out his hand before holding hers longer than necessary. Brook didn't break eye contact. "Did you say that you're investigating a murder?"

"Murders," Brook corrected as she took time to study the layout of the lake house. Oddly enough, the walls were painted a deep charcoal. The dark décor included a smattering of antique furnishings, a leather couch with matching chairs, and mahogany bookshelves positioned on either side of the river-rock fireplace. The masculine interior catered toward fishermen and hunters. "Would you please let Mr. Callaghan know that I'm here?"

"Sure, sure," Cav replied with a crooked smile. He gestured toward the sitting area in the living room. She advanced toward the couch, keeping her credentials in hand. "You said you're with the FBI?"

Brook turned back to face him, though she had not technically ever taken her attention off him. There was something about his interest in her and the case that made her uneasy.

"My firm and I are consulting with the Bureau on an investigation," Brook reiterated as she remained standing in front of the couch. "I'd rather not say anything more until I speak with Mr. Callaghan."

"Of course," Cav stated casually as he turned his head. "Dan! You have a visitor!"

Cav's voice echoed around the room, and Brook was certain that Daniel had heard his friend. A subtle tension settled over the room. She wasn't about to give Cav the attention that he so desired at the moment. There was a suitcase near the bookcase, but she didn't believe the piece of luggage belonged to Cav Buckley. No one who wore such an expensive watch would own cheap luggage.

The sound of footsteps could be heard descending the staircase.

"Did they find my sunglasses?" Dan called out before his loafers hit the main level. His eyes narrowed when he correctly sensed that her visit had nothing to do with lost sunglasses.

"Sorry. I thought one of the renters along the lake found my sunglasses. How can I help you?"

"Brooklyn Sloane," Cav introduced, apparently staying for the upcoming conversation. He had widened his stance and even crossed his arms. "She's working with the FBI on some murder investigation."

"Murder?" Dan's eyebrows raised with disbelief. "Why do you want to speak with me?"

"You had dinner and some drinks at the Crestlake Bar & Grill last weekend," Brook stated as she studied Daniel Callaghan. He had crossed the room and motioned for her to take a seat on the couch. She accepted the invitation after tucking her credentials into the side pocket of her purse. "I was hoping you could walk me through the evening."

Cav, who had been watching the exchange from a respectful distance, finally made his way over. Seeing as Brook had taken the first cushion of the couch, she had done so while making sure there was very little space between her knees and the coffee table. She had also placed her purse on the middle cushion.

"Dan," Cav said with a laugh. "What the hell did you do?"

"Nothing," Daniel replied defensively, leaning forward to rest his elbows on his knees. He opened his hands, palms facing Brook, while he attempted to explain himself. "I was drunk—more than I should have been. Look, Ms. Sloane, there is no excuse for my behavior last Saturday night. I was eventually escorted to the parking lot where a driver brought me back here. I walked to the pier the next morning and picked up my rental car. That's all. I didn't hurt anyone, and I certainly didn't kill anyone."

"Trust me, Dan has trouble gutting a fish," Cav spoke up as he walked over to stand next to his friend. Cav even patted Dan's shoulder in support, although it was clear to Brook that Dan didn't appreciate the character analysis. "I have to ask...is this about Mary Jane Reynolds? We were all talking about her video earlier this week. It's crazy that three women named Mary Jane Reynolds were murdered across the state of Michigan. Was the one who posted the video killed? Is that why you're here?"

"The Mary Jane Reynolds who posted the video is alive and well, but she was the one you interacted with last Saturday, Mr. Callaghan." Brook had spoken directly to Daniel. She came very close to requesting Cav Buckley leave the room. One, she didn't appreciate his repeated attempts to insert himself into the conversation. Second, she genuinely didn't care for his demeanor. "You should know upfront that you are not a suspect. We're aware that you have been working in Detroit on a contracted job through your company for the past six months."

"You could have led with that," Dan replied with a sigh of relief as he leaned back in his chair. He smoothed down the sides of his beard, though nothing was going to tame the mangy hairs. "Why are you here then? If you know that I had nothing to do with the murders, why seek me out?"

"Did you notice anyone paying special attention to Miss Reynolds last Saturday night?" Brook had intentionally not led with the information Bit had given her earlier this morning regarding Dan's alibis. In times of stress, she found that a person's coping mechanism often led them to divulge details that they may not have remembered otherwise. "Maybe someone at the bar? On one of the boats?"

"I had a lot to drink that night," Dan admitted once more as if he relied on that excuse a lot. "Look, I'm going through a real nasty divorce and—"

"That's an understatement," Cav interjected before inadvertently handing her more information about his life. "I'm his divorce attorney. You should see the list of demands that—"

"Were you drunk when you arrived at the pier?" Brook asked Dan, never taking her gaze off him. "I'm assuming you didn't start drinking until you sat at a table. Something about Miss Reynolds caught your attention, though."

"Well, she and her boyfriend didn't seem too happy." Dan appeared hesitant to give up such information, but when Brook didn't alter her expression, he relaxed enough to continue. "The guy was at the bar most of the night."

"That guy is Miss Reynolds' fiancé. Would you mind clarifying exactly what took place between them?"

"Only you would hit on a woman about to get married," Cav said with another short laugh. "And one in the crosshairs of a killer to boot. You take home the prize this time around, Dan."

"About halfway through my dinner, the two of them started arguing about how much she was drinking," Dan responded, ignoring his friend. "She got mad, they exchanged words, and the guy walked over to the bar. He sat on a stool most of the night while she enjoyed time with her friends."

"How many people were at the table?" Brook inquired with curiosity. She made a mental note to speak with Mary Four later in the day. There was a good chance that someone in her group of friends had taken notice of someone suspicious hanging around for the past couple of weeks. "Three? Four?"

"Five, if you count her fiancé."

"Getting back to my initial inquiry, did you notice anyone paying special attention to Miss Reynolds?"

"No."

"Did anyone else interact with the individuals at the table?"

"Mostly just the glances from other folks when the two of them were arguing, but nothing out of the ordinary." Dan paused, as if recalling specific details of that night were difficult. Brook shot a warning glance in Cav's direction when he almost certainly would have filled the void. "One of the other women at the table joined the guy at the bar, though. She had light brown hair that came to her chin."

Brook wouldn't be able to confirm the identity of the woman until a conversation was had with Mary Four, but Dan had described Cindy Reynolds. She had brown hair with blonde highlights, causing the strands to appear light brown in nature. She was most likely trying to mend the argument between her sister and Adam.

"I appreciate your time this morning, Mr. Callaghan." Brook stood as she pulled a business card from the pocket in her blazer. She held it out for him to take. "If you think of anything else from that night, I would appreciate a phone call."

Daniel had followed her lead, pushing himself out of the chair. He perused the information on the card before tucking it into the back pocket of his jeans. The differences between the two men were substantial, and Brook was curious as to the other occupants of the house.

"Just to confirm, you were alone at the Crestlake Bar & Grill last weekend, correct?"

"Yeah," Dan replied with a nod, gesturing toward his friend. "Cav couldn't join us until Monday. Steve's flight was delayed a day by those fires out West, and he didn't arrive until Sunday afternoon. Steve and I have flights out tonight, while Cav doesn't drive home until tomorrow."

"Steve lives on the West Coast?" Brook asked casually as she began to make her way toward the front door. She had caught sight of the kitchen behind Cav, noting the stack of poker chips and two decks of cards on the table. "I heard some areas had to evacuate."

"Steve lives north of the fire, but the heavy smoke closed most of the airports." Cav had chosen to answer her questions and follow behind her, basically inserting himself between her and Dan. "Listen, since I'm going to be in town until tomorrow, would you care to have a drink with me?"

"I'm going to have to decline, Mr. Buckley." By the time that Brook had finished her sentence, she was mere inches from the screen door. She turned to find Cav's dark eyes fixed on the lower part of her body. She purposefully cleared her throat until his gaze met hers. "Enjoy the rest of your stay."

Brook gave a respectful nod toward Dan, who stood maybe ten feet away from his friend. The screen door closed with a soft click behind her. There were no shadows on the ground since the sun was currently tucked behind the overhead clouds. It seemed as if the storm front had moved in faster than the meteorologists had predicted, but she figured she still had about half an hour before the rain arrived.

She had already reached into her purse and pulled out the key fob. Once she had unlocked the van, she opened the driver's side door, discreetly taking in her surroundings. Dan had mentioned that Cav was driving home tomorrow, and one of the two vehicles in the driveway happened to be a rental car, leaving the other one with Michigan plates to belong to Cav Buckley.

Brook had set her purse on the passenger seat. Her phone was in the side pocket, and she was able to retrieve it with little fuss. She accessed her speed dial list and gently pressed down on Bit's name. It wasn't a surprise when he answered on the first ring.

"I need you to run a background check for me," Brook said as she started the engine. Cav Buckley was still observing her from behind the screen door. The way he had interjected himself into the conversation had left her uncomfortable with his interest. She rattled off the man's license plate number. "It's probably nothing, but I want everything you can find on Cav Buckley. Oh, and a male subject named Steve joined Callaghan and Buckley for the week. I'd like a background check run on him, too."

"Anything else, Boss?"

"Yes," Brook replied slowly as she thought over the details that Daniel had given her from last weekend. "Adam Bouras. I read over his background check last night, but would you mind conducting a deeper dive on social media? I'd like to know exactly how dedicated he is to his fiancé."

CHAPTER NINE

Sylvie Deering

May 2024

Saturday — 1:03 pm

THE DISTANT RUMBLE OF thunder could be heard traveling across the grey clouds overhead. The vibrations became so deep that they eventually rattled the windows of the kitchen. Severe weather was rolling across the state of Michigan, and the storm was slowly approaching the city of Lansing. Such a dark ambiance wasn't the most ideal setting in which Sylvie would have preferred to speak with Duncan Reynolds.

"Would you like some coffee?" Duncan asked as he gestured toward the island in the kitchen. There were three stools tucked in underneath the lip of a light grey granite countertop. "I just brewed a fresh pot."

Duncan Reynolds had been married to the second victim for a little over nine years. The house that they had chosen to purchase two years after their wedding was a two-story residence located at the end of a cul-de-sac surrounded by tall oak trees. The main level had an open layout, and Sylvie was able to take in not only the kitchen but also the living room and dining room. Their chosen décor radiated warmth and comfort by merging several earth tones together.

"Yes," Sylvie replied, pulling out a stool so that it was diagonal to the counter. She wanted a chance to survey the living room, which was where Mary Jane's body had been found on the floor with several stab wounds to her chest. "Thank you."

Sylvie didn't prefer coffee, but allowing Duncan to undertake a task would afford him some semblance of control. She wouldn't even take one sip of the hot beverage during her visit. She had learned long ago from Theo to never drink anything given to her by a witness or suspect. Considering that Duncan Reynolds had a solid alibi for the night his wife was killed, he fell into the first category.

"I hope it's alright that my daughter isn't here." Duncan turned around with two cups of coffee. He slid one over to her, but he remained standing on the other side of the island. The way his knuckles tightened around the mug displayed his desire to be anywhere else but here with her. "Ava slept through...well, she didn't see anything that night. It took close to two months before my daughter felt comfortable enough to go to a friend's house without me. I didn't want anything that we might say to one another setting her back any."

Considering that Mary Two had been murdered in January, Sylvie wouldn't have wanted Ava to relive such a tragic moment, either. Sylvie's visit wasn't intended to disrupt their grieving process. On the other hand, speaking with the victim's husband four months after her death could shed some light on any details that he might have remembered since then. While usually it was best to take statements right after a crime, there were times that minute details weren't recalled until something triggered them during the witness' daily routines.

"I have Ava's statement from that night," Sylvie replied softly as she waited for Duncan to join her at the counter. She was hoping that he would change his mind, but he seemed more comfortable with the distance between them. "Since the FBI has taken on the investigation, my colleagues and I thought it best to speak with the victims' family members and friends. We believe it's important to know Mary Jane Reynolds...all of them."

Sylvie paused when Duncan dropped his gaze. He swallowed a few times, indicating that he was struggling to keep his emotions in check.

"Your Mary Jane, Duncan." Sylvie needed him to understand how vital it was for him to share the details of their lives. "Tell me about your wife."

"Her laughter was contagious," Duncan replied with a small smile, though it didn't reach his eyes. He stared into his mug as if he could visualize his memories in the dark beverage. "Mary was kind, funny, and...loved cheese."

Duncan laughed before shaking his head.

"I know that isn't what you want to know, but Mary loved cheese. She passed that on to our daughter, too. Ava will eat anything and everything, as long as I melt cheese over it." Duncan shrugged in defeat, albeit good-naturedly. He lifted his mug to his lips and took a long sip. "You want to know if Mary had any enemies, and the answer is no. Everyone loved her, with the exception of Mrs. Johnston across the street. That woman doesn't like any of her neighbors."

There were two entrances within sight from the majority of the main level—the front entrance, which Sylvie had walked through after parking the car near the curb out front, and the back door located in the kitchen. There had been no signs of forced entry, and none of the doorbell cameras in the neighborhood had caught anything suspicious that evening. The local police believed that Mary Jane had invited her murderer into the house, but that scenario couldn't have taken place. There had been no prints left behind to indicate a visitor, either. The odd thing Sylvie had noted in the detective's files was that the surfaces in the house hadn't been wiped down.

"What about someone new?" Sylvie inquired as she turned the warm mug in her hand. "Did either of you meet someone new in the weeks leading up to that night? I know that Mary was a high school teacher. Did she mention someone new at school?"

Sylvie had noticed right away that Duncan didn't refer to his wife as Mary Jane. He called her Mary, and Sylvie would respect the manner in which he would like to remember his wife.

"There were a couple of new substitute teachers who started filling in for the full-time teachers back in January. There's usually an influx when a new semester starts." Duncan lifted one corner of his lips in thought before he continued with more specifics. "A young guy in his twenties, and a woman in her sixties. I remember that conversation vividly, because Mary was saying the older woman had the patience of a saint."

Sylvie made a mental note to request background checks on both colleagues. After a few more questions without any new details that weren't in the reports, Sylvie switched gears.

"Would you please walk me through that day?" Sylvie maintained a delicate tone, knowing how difficult doing so would be for Duncan.

"It started out as any other morning." Duncan set his mug on the counter before crossing his arms over his chest. "Our alarm went off around a quarter after six. Mary jumped in the shower while I went to make breakfast for Ava. I swear that girl has an internal clock. She was already dressed by the time I walked past her bedroom, but she couldn't find her favorite pair of socks."

"Let me guess," Sylvie said with a soft smile to keep Duncan somewhat in the present. It wouldn't do to completely lose him in the past. "Ava's socks were in the dirty laundry."

"They were," Duncan replied with a tender smile. "I ended up tossing them in the dryer with a dryer sheet while Ava ate her favorite cereal. By the time I had returned to the bathroom to brush my teeth, Mary was already out of the shower and getting dressed. There was nothing unusual about our morning routine."

"What time did the three of you leave the house?"

"Seven-thirty," Duncan responded at the same time that his phone chimed an incoming text. He didn't hesitate to pick his cell up off the counter. Sylvie assumed that his daughter wasn't the one reaching out to him, because he set his phone down without responding to the message. "I kissed both of them goodbye. Ava hopped into her booster seat and fastened her seatbelt while Mary settled in behind the steering wheel. We both park in the garage, so I waited until she pulled out before getting into my car."

Sylvie had caught Duncan's slip of speaking about his wife in the present tense, but that wasn't unusual during interviews like this one.

"When you pulled out of the driveway, did you notice any unusual vehicles parked on the street?"

"Not that I can recall." Duncan had crossed his arms once again, but he lifted his right hand to rub his thumb across his chin. Typically, such a gesture indicated the individual wasn't being truthful, but Sylvie had recognized early on that it was his way of soothing himself. "I always make sure the garage door closes all the way, so I was focused on that while letting the car idle in the driveway. By the time that I had pulled onto the street, Mary had already left the neighborhood."

"You work at a doctor's office, correct? An RN?" Sylvie asked, already knowing the answer to her question. Her inquiry was merely to keep the memories fresh in Duncan's mind. "Did you drive straight there? Stop off for coffee?"

"I didn't stop anywhere that morning." Duncan dropped his hand to rest on his other arm. His movement indicated that he was subconsciously aware nothing out of the ordinary happened the rest of the day. "Since Mary teaches at the high school, it's easier for her to drop Ava off at the elementary school. I used to work twelve-hour shifts at the hospital, but not after Ava was born. I wanted something with fewer hours so that I could be home in the evening. The only day of the week that we have longer office hours is Thursday. Dr. Roberts sees patients until around six or so."

Mary Two had been murdered on a Thursday, but according to the criminal report, the late office hours hadn't been the reason that Duncan hadn't been at home that evening.

"Did you speak with Mary at any point throughout the day?"

"Yes," Duncan replied with a nod. "Mary always calls on her way home. She had picked up Ava, who had gotten an A on her spelling test, and they were stopping to pick up a pizza. Since I'm usually not home for dinner on Thursday nights, it became a habit to eat take-out food."

"Nothing was said during the course of the phone conversation that caused you to think something was wrong?"

"No, nothing," Duncan replied before glancing toward the back door of the kitchen when another roll of thunder materialized outside. "I know that Mary picked up the pizza, because I spoke to her on the phone again about five minutes after I left the clinic. She and Ava had already eaten, and they were about to play Candyland. I was maybe five minutes from home when I got a call from the alarm company. I'm second on the list, and the operator couldn't get ahold of Dr. Roberts. The police were already responding to the call, so I had no choice but to turn around and drive back to work."

"It's my understanding that Dr. Roberts was driving to a restaurant to meet his wife, but he had forgotten to take his cell phone off silent," Sylvie tacked on to confirm what was in Dr. Benjamin Roberts' statement. "He arrived at his clinic around fifteen minutes after you, correct?"

"Yes. We have at least one break-in a year, if not two. It's not uncommon. Unfortunately, there is always someone looking for a way to score drugs. We don't keep narcotics on hand, though."

"Was anything taken?"

"A few samples from our sample drawers were raided, but our security company is outstanding," Duncan replied before giving his opinion on the robbery. "The detective doesn't believe the break-in had anything to do with my wife's murder. I'm inclined to agree, because that would mean someone went to a lot of trouble to make sure that I wasn't home that night. I just...I can't wrap my head around that."

"How long were you at the clinic that night?"

"The police finished taking statements from me and Dr. Roberts around eight o'clock. I stayed behind for another forty minutes or so to organize the mess left behind." Duncan inhaled slowly as he ventured ahead with his story of what was waiting for him at home. "I pulled into the garage. Mary's SUV was parked in its usual spot. I made sure the garage door was closed before walking into the mudroom. I was quiet since I knew that Ava's bedtime was around seven-thirty. I made my way through the kitchen, expecting Mary to be grading papers in the living room. She loved listening to music on low and enjoying a glass of wine while sitting in front of the fireplace."

"Did you hear music when you entered the house?"

Sylvie's question grabbed Duncan's attention. The way his eyes narrowed and the manner in which he focused his attention on the black box near the television emphasized his struggle to recall such a detail. He gradually shook his head.

"No. No, there wasn't any music playing," Duncan replied as his stare drifted toward the overstuffed chair closest to the gas fireplace. "I do remember that Mary's tablet and stylus were on the side table next to the chair."

"And a wineglass?"

Duncan once again shook his head in response.

"I take it that grading papers with a glass of wine and some music was a nightly ritual for Mary?" Sylvie asked, hoping to pinpoint a smaller timeframe so that Bit could once again go through a specific range of security footage obtained from the neighbors' doorbell cameras. "Did she do so at a certain time?"

"After tucking Ava into bed, which is around seven-thirty."

Sylvie granted another fifteen minutes for Mary to have picked up a bit, maybe place some dishes in the dishwasher, before she collected her tablet from her purse or bag. No music or wine meant that someone had come into the home before Mary had been able to finish setting the ambiance for a comfortable evening. Still, nothing that Bit had discovered on the footage handed over by the local police had shown anyone near the front of the house.

"Mr. Reynolds, would you mind if I take a walk around your backyard?" Sylvie asked after listening to the details of how he had discovered his wife's body lying on the area rug. Mary had changed into loungewear at some point during the evening, and her light grey long-sleeved shirt had been soaked in blood. Duncan immediately dialed 911 after checking for a pulse. He described the sightless eyes of his wife, and how he had known instantly that no measures taken could have saved her life. "The detective made several references in his report that there were no forced signs of entry on the doors or windows. No one's security cameras caught anyone of interest out front, but aerial footage shows a conservation area out back."

"We had snow in January, and there were no footprints from the side gate to the back door," Duncan responded as he shifted his weight to push off the counter.

Sylvie left her now cold coffee on the countertop as she stood from the stool to follow him. He flipped the deadbolt and opened the back door. Lightning branched across the sky, its brief illumination displaying the gathered storm clouds above.

Sylvie figured she had mere minutes before raindrops began to fall.

"Mary wouldn't have let some stranger inside the house, either."

Sylvie stepped onto the back patio after Duncan had moved to the side. He didn't bother to close the door. Instead, he remained near the threshold as he studied the darkening sky above. The air was charged with humidity even though the storm front was bringing in cooler temperatures.

"Mr. Reynolds, did you have some work done to the landscape recently?"

"As a matter of fact, yes." Duncan leaned a shoulder against the doorframe. He gestured toward the flat gray pavers that served as a walkway toward the side gate. Only there was a more established path that led from the back patio to the conservation area, running horizontally through the backyards behind the row of homes on the north side of the neighborhood. "Mary and I had planned to buy a pontoon boat for the lake, and she was really hung up on making a beautiful pathway lined with flowers between the house and conservation area."

"The pavers that lead to the trees seem to have been there for a while," Sylvie pointed out as she thought back to the crime scene photos. Forensics had taken pictures of the exterior, as well. "Did you or Mary spread salt pebbles over the stones? The notation in the report regarding the assumption that no one had entered the backyard focused on the undisturbed blanket of snow."

"That's because there were no footprints on either side of the house," Duncan responded with a frown. He didn't seem to be on the same page as her. "Granted, the pavers are heated, but there were still no tracks discovered in the snow."

"The pavers are heated?" The first raindrop fell from the gathered clouds above, but Sylvie remained standing on the edge of the patio. "So there wouldn't have been any snow to leave footprints behind on the surface of the pavers then."

"True, but whoever murdered my wife would have had to walk around the house."

"Or entered through the back gate that opens into the conservation area."

Duncan was already shaking his head at Sylvie's theory, but she had witnessed firsthand the lengths a killer would go to in an effort to reach his or her target.

"There are fences on both ends of the conservation area, and the police canvassed the backyards of every home," Duncan revealed somewhat reluctantly, though Sylvie could sense his interest in her theory. "Even if what you say is true, and someone used a boat to reach the conservation area, Mary never would have allowed someone into our home."

"What if a male subject was in trouble? Would Mary have wanted to help him?" Sylvie asked as the spitting of raindrops became more frequent. She finally turned and began to walk back toward Duncan. "What if the man had blood on his head or maybe wet clothes from falling into the lake?"

Duncan hesitated, but Sylvie already had her answer. Mary Two had been a very kind individual, and she never would have let someone hurt remain outside in freezing temperatures. What Sylvie hadn't mentioned was that she believed whoever had been at Mary's back door had been someone she was familiar with...either from school, the local cafe, or maybe even the grocery store.

A clap of thunder was joined by a very long streak of lightning, prompting Sylvie to quicken her pace. She and Duncan entered the house right as the sky opened up and released a deluge of rain. She swept her gaze over the backyard before closing the door against the severe elements. It was one thing to know about the lake and the conservation area, but it was another thing entirely to know about specialty items such as heated pavers to obscure one's footprints.

CHAPTER TEN

Bobby "Bit" Nowacki

May 2024

Saturday — 3:21 pm

THE STORM FRONT WAS set to ease in an hour or two. Until then, the heavy rain and strong winds would continue to currently hammer against the windows. The double panes currently rattled with force as the claps of thunder took a backseat. Fortunately, an adequate amount of the gathering clouds had drifted far enough east to diminish the lightning.

While Bit always took additional precautions with his equipment by using surge protectors, one could never be certain of their effectiveness. The interior of the Airbnb had become so dim during the brunt of the storms that he had been forced to turn on the two lamps that had been placed on the side tables.

Bit had several monitors on the table, each with a specific purpose. One of the screens currently displayed Mary Four's social media profile. As of this morning, she had recorded herself on a live feed thanking her viewers for helping attain the attention of the FBI. She had even mentioned that she had been given twenty-four-seven protection.

The video had prompted Brook to visit the woman earlier this afternoon.

Bit wouldn't hold his breath that Mary Four would listen to Brook's advice when it came to not putting her life on social media. Surprisingly, Adam Bouras had been at the house. He had previously been scheduled to be in Flint, but he claimed that the storms had changed his plans. Brook had managed to discover who Adam's friend was who helped escort Daniel Callaghan to the parking lot, and Adam had been referring to Jason Bracco.

"Boss, Bouras' supervisor confirmed the change in plans," Bit informed Brook as she walked into the living room with a fresh mug of coffee. "Also, Bouras has a soft alibi for Mary Three."

"Soft?" Brook asked as she continued to walk around his makeshift desk. "Not definitive?"

"I put in a request for a warrant to access the hotel's security feed where Bouras was staying that night. Once I confirm that Bouras never left his hotel, then we can cross him off the suspect list."

Bit leaned back in his chair when Brook came to a stop in front of the portable monitor. She had been staring at the data on the screen since she had returned from her visit with Mary Four, which had been at least thirty minutes ago. Brook had taken her blazer off after walking into the house. The holster clipped to her belt was the same one that he was currently using for his firearm. Before working for S&E Investigations, he never would have thought that carrying a weapon would turn into a daily habit.

Sylvie's attempted murder had changed his viewpoint.

Bit adjusted his headphones against his neck when some of his strands had gotten caught underneath the weight. It was interesting that the heaviness on his waist no longer bothered him. He and Sylvie had been to the range numerous times over the last couple of months, and he was more comfortable now than ever before.

A soft chime came from one of his monitors, causing him to push the soles of his shoes against the hard plastic mat that he had laid down before bringing in the long table, rolling chairs, computers, and all the accessories. He scanned the results of an application that he had run from cell phone data provided by the victims' providers.

"There were no overlapping calls placed or received by the victims from their cell phones," Bit informed her as he tabbed to the next screen. "No text messages or DMs overlapped, either."

"I'm not surprised," Brook murmured before she lifted the mug to her lips. As usual, her long black hair hung over her left shoulder. The strands were so dark that the color became almost one with her long-sleeved black blouse. "Nothing else has matched up, yet the manner of death the unsub has chosen is very personal."

"Nothing like being stabbed to death," Bit muttered under his breath as he reached for his soft drink.

While he loved his energy drinks, he liked to mix it up once in a while. The orange bubbles were a refreshing change of pace. By the time he set the can back down on the table, Brook was lost in her own world. He was always amazed by how her mind worked, but he was also aware of the reason behind such an ability to profile others.

Bit took a moment to glance at Mary Four's social media profile again. Even though Brook had warned the woman this afternoon about putting too much information online, it was doubtful that she would listen to such advice.

"Why the shoulder blade?" Brook's question came out of the blue, but Bit was used to the figurative inquiries. She probably already had an answer queued up. "Mary One and Mary Two were both stabbed in the chest. The autopsies confirmed it was the same type of knife used on all three victims, if not the same knife. Mary Three was attacked from behind, but it was only after she fell to the ground and turned on her back that the unsub delivered the fatal puncture wound."

"Mary Three was jogging," Bit chimed in right as his cell phone signaled that he had an incoming text. Since he had diverted his messages to his main laptop, he clicked on the images that Arden had sent seconds ago. "What if Mary Three noticed that she was being followed and attempted to run faster? Maybe the unsub tackled her from behind. Not thinking he had a choice, he stabbed her in the back so she wouldn't get away."

"Considering the bruises and scrapes discovered on Mary Three's hands and knees, that could be an accurate assumption." Brook closed the distance to the touchscreen monitor and pulled up the medical examiner's file. The photographs caused Bit to glance down at his keyboard. "Or she simply stumbled forward from the force of the blow."

Bit gave Brook about three minutes to study Mary Three's injuries before he pressed a button on his keyboard. Soon, those grisly pictures were replaced with a series of cute and innocent images as they popped up on the screen one at a time.

A white kitten with crystal blue eyes had been caught in adorable poses raising her paw toward the lens. She was captured closer to the phone each time. Bit wasn't usually sappy, but he found it difficult not to be all gushy at the sight of such a pristine ball of fur. Arden had also attached a video, and Bit began to play it before Brook could stop him.

The tiny kitten, all fluff and paws, was fiercely battling a pink ball. The silver bell inside jingled with each swipe, which only enticed the kitten to continue her daring pursuit. Either that, or it was Arden's encouraging words in the background. Bit was pretty sure it was the twitch of the kitten's whiskers that caused Brook to finally break down and smile.

"I think Arden is going to have a tough time handing over that handful of energy."

"Considering how much we travel, Gumshoe will definitely get some quality time with the furball," Bit said as he replayed the video. It was a nice change of pace to witness Brook soften her stance. He would never say such a thing out loud, but the color of her irises matched that of the kitten's eyes. "What do you think Little T will name her? Snowball?"

"Knowing Sylvie, she'll think outside the box." Brook's smile faded slowly as Bit closed out of the video and made sure there were no traces of the images for Sylvie to find once she got back from Lansing. "Speaking of Sylvie, she's not driving back until Monday. She wants to speak with the staff of the high school, along with Ava Reynolds' teacher at the lower school."

"And Big T?"

"Returning tonight." Brook stood in such a way that it afforded her the ability to study the screen and carry on a conversation with him. "What did you find on the substitute teacher?"

Bit had rolled his chair to position himself back in front of the computer that he was previously working on, lines of codes shifting and scrolling with precision. He was pleased with the program that should produce results on whether there had been any social media crossover with the victims. His first program had yielded nothing, but he had been able to adjust some parameters that would confirm the previous results.

"The substitute teacher is Eric Langdon," Bit said before minimizing the code window to reveal the man's profile. With a press of a button, the information materialized on the portable monitor. "Twenty-nine years of age with a bachelor's degree in education. His minor was in history, but he has yet to land a full-time position with the school. Langdon grew up in the area, graduated from that particular high school, and his father still lives in the same house."

"Mother?"

Bit wasn't surprised in the least that Brook focused on Langdon's maternal parent. Most serial killers had issues with their mothers, and their victims tended to share the same maternal traits. Langdon didn't fit in with those types of individuals, though.

"Langdon's mother was never in the picture. She died from an aneurysm the day after giving birth to him." Bit made sure that the mother's name was highlighted on the screen. "Her name was Abagail Rose."

"Does Langdon have alibis for the three dates in question?"

"Two out of the three," Bit replied as another alert caught his attention. "Langdon doesn't like social media, so it's difficult to know about the day that Mary Two was murdered."

"And Mary Two is the Mary Jane Reynolds who knew him personally," Brook said softly before walking toward the couch. She had kicked off her high heels upon entering the house earlier, so she was able to tuck her feet underneath her as she made herself comfortable on the cushion. Her tablet had been on the arm of the couch, and it didn't take her long to settle in to read the latest notes entered by Sylvie and Theo. "Sylvie will be able to press Langdon on Monday. In the meantime, we'll continue to search for a connection between the victims. It's there. We just need to find it."

Bit remained silent as he read over an email that wasn't directed at him. He adjusted his knitted hat after the third read-through.

"Bit, spit it out."

Bit glanced to the left of the monitor, noting that Brook's attention was on the tablet instead of him. She had a knack for knowing when something was wrong, but he doubted that she was ready to hear what he had to say about Jacob.

"It's probably nothing."

"If it was nothing, then you wouldn't have lost color in your face."

Bit was well aware that he had pale features, partly due to his genetics and the other part because he preferred to stay indoors behind his screens. Besides, he remembered to take supplements now and then in case of any vitamin deficiencies.

When he didn't reply right away, Brook finally switched her attention from the tablet to him. She was the most difficult person to read in any situation. Now was no exception. He sensed that she had braced herself for what he was about to reveal, but he couldn't be certain.

Monitoring government systems wasn't the wisest thing to do when he was on their radar, but risks had to be taken when it came to Brook's brother. Seeing as Bit swept his space every morning, as well as ran his own programmed scan of any devices being used on a daily basis, it was doubtful that the FBI was listening in on their conversation.

Still, he was always careful with what he said aloud.

"Did you hear about the outbreak at the federal prison?" Bit asked casually, though he wasn't sure that he had pulled off such an attitude. "Influenza A, apparently. A few of the prisoners were transferred to a local hospital."

"Such an article hasn't come across my newsfeed, but I can see why the subject would garner interest from the press," Brook responded in a measured tone. She casually stood from the cushion, leaving her tablet on the arm of the couch. She picked up her phone instead. "I should probably make a few phone calls."

Bit continued to tap his thumb against the table as Brook left the living room. The inbox that he had been monitoring belonged to the warden of the federal prison where Jacob was being held, and Bit had set up a program where keywords were tagged...such as *transport*. There were a couple of names listed in the body of the email, but Jacob's name had not been one of them. The hospital would have sectioned off a wing of the hospital to avoid any threats to the other patients. Guards would also be stationed in and around the hospital depending on the prisoner.

Regardless, the team needed to take the necessary precautions to guarantee Jacob's name was never added to such a list. Bit couldn't hear Brook's side of the phone conversation, but he was certain that the topic of solitary confinement would be part of the discussion. Only time would reveal if such a request had been made before possible exposure to the virus.

CHAPTER ELEVEN

Brooklyn Sloane

May 2024

Monday — 2:48 pm

THE CRISP, EVENING BREEZE swept across the lake, leaving Brook wishing she had worn her blazer while speaking with Graham on the back deck. Ever since the storms left the area on Saturday, a cool snap had remained behind. Unfortunately, Graham might be doing the same in Somalia, leaving his mother to celebrate her birthday alone. He hadn't informed his mother yet, though he assured Brook that Elizabeth would be fine either way. She was quite active in the social circles of D.C.

Brook stared across the lake at the pier. Even for a Monday night, the Crestlake Bar & Grill was doing quite the business. Most of the tables were full, and she figured it was a mixture of locals and tourists. There didn't seem to be anyone alone, which was how Elizabeth's birthday could potentially be spent if Brook didn't fly back to the city Wednesday morning.

Forcing that decision to the back of her mind, she kept ahold of her phone as she turned to walk across the deck. She opened the sliding glass door, ensuring that the lock was engaged before she continued across the kitchen. Delicious aromas wafted from the living room where the team was enjoying their meals. She had kept them waiting long enough.

"...knew the family well enough to know that the Reynolds had heated pavers installed in the backyard." Sylvie glanced toward Brook as she entered the room. "Bit said that he'll see if any of the homes on the other side of the lake have any security systems installed facing the water. If so, there is a chance that we can capture someone accessing the small pier on the opposite side of the conservation area from Mary Two's residence."

Sylvie was sitting in the overstuffed chair with her bare feet propped up on the matching ottoman. In her lap was a container that held a handful of fries. A single glimpse at Theo and Bit sitting at the table confirmed that they had also polished off their meals. After Brook's conversation with Graham, she wasn't all that hungry.

"I was thinking about your visit to Lansing after our discussion," Brook said, directing her statement toward Sylvie. The two of them had spent a good half hour after Sylvie returned from her trip this afternoon discussing the intel gathered from the husband and Mary Two's colleagues. "You might want to video conference with Duncan Reynolds to show him a photograph of Adam Bouras. See if Reynolds has ever spoken to Bouras."

"No need, Boss. The hotel manager sent me hallway footage of the fourth floor," Bit chimed in as he reached for the drink that had come with his meal. From the slurping sound, it didn't appear that there was any soda left in the cup. "Bouras never left his room the night that Mary Three was murdered, so he now has solid alibis for all three murders."

"Your fish and chips dinner is on the coffee table," Theo shared as he leaned back in his chair. He used a napkin to wipe his fingers after eating his last shrimp. "Mindy put in an extra side of barbeque sauce."

"One of us really needs to take a cooking class," Sylvie murmured as she picked up another fry and stared at it with a frown. "Seriously, eating out every day like this when we're in the field is bad for our arteries."

"Gumshoe said he survived on hot dogs from the street vendors during his stint as a PI. Burgers and fries have to be better than hot dogs, right?"

Bit's statement even had Brook staring at him in horror.

"Well, we know who isn't going to take a cooking class," Theo said wryly as he tossed his crumpled napkin into his empty container. He then closed the lid before reaching for his water. "On a serious note, I did speak with Hunter Darrisaw. He had nothing new to add that Mindy, Chip, and Jason hadn't already revealed about Daniel Callaghan. As for my trip to Mount Pleasant, Mary Three's parents had no idea if Mary Three had met someone new. The victim pretty much led her own life while living at home and saving enough money to move out on her own. No new colleagues, no new routines...nothing. Bit looked into delivery people, both at the victim's home and workplace. Nothing stands out."

"Anything on Cav Buckley?" Brook had already read over the man's background check, but Bit had been going to perform a deeper dive into the man's social media presence. "His interest in the case seemed a little extreme."

"Must be the lawyer in him, because Buckley is clean. He has alibis for all three murders," Bit said as he began to scan the room. "Did we get dessert?"

Theo muttered something about Bit being a bottomless pit causing Sylvie to laugh.

"My purse is behind you. I stopped at the gas station to top off the tank," Sylvie said as she closed the lid to her container. "Throw me the chocolate bar."

"Have I taught you nothing?" Theo asked Sylvie in disbelief.

"Your advice has been invaluable to my recovery, Theo," Sylvie said sincerely as she held up her hands to catch the candy bar. Bit hadn't wasted any time fishing out the treats. "But do we need to go over the moderation thing again? I haven't had chocolate in a week."

Not even Brook could make such an admission.

"Could the husband have orchestrated his wife's murder?" Theo asked to bring the conversation back around to the investigation. "Perhaps the other murders were a smokescreen for his own crime?"

"Unlikely," Sylvie replied as she began to peel back the wrapper. "He was surrounded by cops at the clinic that night."

"Did the police ever make an arrest?" Brook asked with curiosity as she took a seat on the couch. "It was certainly convenient that the husband wasn't home that night."

"Meaning someone staged it?" Sylvie nodded her agreement after a moment of consideration. "I could see that being the case, especially given that we believe the unsub had prior knowledge of the heated pavers. If we go with that assumption, the unsub would have also known that their daughter's bedtime was around seven-thirty. Interestingly enough, an arrest in the clinic's break-in was never made."

"Bit, would you please request access to the security footage for the clinic that night?" Brook took time to mentally calculate the time needed for such a premeditated murder. "If there was a boat readily available to the unsub, the timeline would work in that theory."

The team spent another half an hour covering the intel gathered over the past four days, but there hadn't been much progress in the grand scheme of things. Granted, every individual ruled out as the unsub was a small step forward, but they needed some lead to propel them forward.

"Theo, you walked the route Mary Three took while jogging that evening, right?" Brook had kept a crime scene photo of Mary Three up on the portable monitor. "Did you notice anything unusual about the area? The trees seem sparse, not leaving a lot of room for the unsub to camouflage himself."

"You're interested in why Mary Three was stabbed in the back," Theo commented as his gaze remained on the large screen. "I've been thinking a lot about that too. And to answer your question, no. There wasn't a lot of coverage, so we can assume that he came up to her from behind."

"What if the unsub was with her?" Brook murmured more to herself. "We believe the unsub is somehow inserting himself into his victims' lives. If the unsub was running alongside her, slowed just enough to let her edge ahead, he could have easily stabbed her."

"The autopsy report for Mary Three did indicate that the stab wound was practically straightforward," Sylvie recalled after taking a bite of her chocolate bar. "The unsub would be right-handed in that case."

"There are no security cameras on the trail where Mary Three took her daily jog," Bit said as he opened the bag of Skittles that Sylvie had purchased for him. He picked out a couple of red ones before holding up a finger. "I could try and find traffic cams that point to her parents' neighborhood. Someone could have followed her from there."

"One of us is going to need to drive to Ann Arbor," Brook stated as she spun the outer band of her worry ring. Doing so helped her concentrate on the screen. "According to my profile, the unsub would have chosen these victims based on the ease of reaching them. I don't necessarily believe they were murdered in some meaningful order."

"You always say the answer lies with the first victim," Sylvie pointed out as she began to close the wrapper around the other half of her chocolate bar. She hadn't been kidding about everything in moderation. "Mary Four's online plea was what brought us here, and the pressure from the FBI didn't help our situation. Maybe we should be concentrating our investigation in another city."

"It was my decision to begin our investigation here versus Ann Arbor." Brook wasn't the type of woman who didn't own up to her mistakes, and she took full responsibility for the direction of the case. "The profile points to the unsub observing his victims for weeks at a time. Mary Four's video should have brought him here."

"Your profiles have yet to steer us wrong," Theo pointed out as he reached for his empty container. Bit rolled off the clear plastic mat until he could reach the grandfather clock behind him. He knocked on the side while shooting Theo a glare. "Do I even want to know what that was for?"

"I'm knocking on wood." Bit used the soles of his shoes to drag himself back onto the mat before parking himself in front of his favorite laptop. He then picked up his take-out container and handed it over to Theo since he was collecting the garbage. "You can't tempt fate like that, man."

The jogging trail was still an anomaly that Brook couldn't wrap her mind around.

"The slight difference in the stab wounds in Mary Three's case is significant. It bothers me." Brook moved toward the kitchen, picking up her uneaten dinner. She needed more time to think through the abnormalities that took place with the third victim. "Let's take the evening to consider our next steps. We'll decide in the morning who should make the drive to Ann Arbor."

After promising Sylvie that Brook would put the tea kettle on one of the burners, she followed Theo into the kitchen. She retrieved a plate from the cupboard and a fork from the drawer before she began to transfer the contents of her meal. She didn't want to take the chance that the plastic would melt in the microwave, even though there was a label stating the opposite.

"I'm sure Bit filled you in on what is taking place at the prison." Brook tossed the empty container into the garbage can. "Once I reached the warden, he said that he didn't call me because the prisoners were located in another cell block."

"Did you request that Jacob be moved to solitary confinement?"

"Yes." Brook programmed the time on the keypad and then leaned back against the counter after the microwave hummed to life. "The average incubation for Influenza A is about two days, but it can take up to four. Under normal circumstances, this wouldn't be an issue."

"Exactly. The likelihood that anyone, let alone Jacob, would need to be transported to the hospital is rare. The prison has its own medical facilities, Brook." Theo turned on the faucet to wash his hands. "Why were the prisoners transferred to the hospital to begin with?"

"Dehydration, difficulty breathing, and so on." Brook ran through the conversation that she had with the warden. "From what I'm being told, the infirmary was at capacity, so the prison transferred the more critical patients. Two of those patients are in their late seventies."

Brook held up her hand, knowing full well that Theo was about to run down the odds of Jacob becoming so sick that he would need to be transferred to a hospital. She understood that the probability was low, but she would never alter her stance of being prepared for anything.

"I'm going to stop by the federal prison Wednesday morning."

"You're flying back to D.C.?"

"Yes," Brook replied over the microwave's peal. She sensed the weight of Theo's stare as she turned to pull on the handle. "I'll touch base with Arden in the morning regarding my plans.

Considering we're in a regrouping phase in the investigation anyway, I might as well take advantage of the lull."

While there were no federal prisons located in Washington, D.C., Brook had pulled some strings to transfer Jacob to a federal prison in Maryland. The facility was a little over two hours from D.C., but she would have enough time to drive there and back in time for dinner.

"And you'll be back...when?"

Theo was fishing for information on whether she was going to remain in the city to celebrate Elizabeth Elliott's birthday.

"Thursday."

Theo knocked shoulders with her in silent victory. It was a good thing that Brook had already set her plate on the counter. She tried not to smile, but that was rather difficult when he started singing one of his favorite songs about being unstoppable at the top of his lungs. He had figured out relatively quickly that she had taken his advice. Before too long, Brook could hear Sylvie and Bit joining in from the other room just for fun.

As Theo practically danced out of the kitchen with an undeniable rhythm, Brook remained at the counter to eat her dinner. Hearing their voices get even louder, she couldn't deny that it was nice to have things back to normal. Unfortunately, in her experience, those times never lasted long.

CHAPTER TWELVE

Brooklyn Sloane

May 2024

Wednesday — 5:57 pm

THE UPSCALE DINING ESTABLISHMENT in downtown D.C. buzzed with low murmurs of the city's elite. The warm glow of the subtle overhead lighting cast faint shadows across the sleek black leather chairs and crisp white tablecloths. The wall panels were made of rich mahogany, and the dark wood was offset by the delicate lightbulbs encased in wrought iron fixtures. Each specific detail had been thought out to the nth degree, and it was obvious that this was not one's average dining experience.

Brook's high heels clicked softly on the wooden floor as she made her way across the large foyer to the hostess stand. A young woman was speaking with an older gentleman who was requesting something special for his wife. Brook didn't mind the short pause in her evening. Such an opportunity to gather her thoughts and take a much-needed calming breath had been few and far between in the past twenty-four hours.

Arden had scheduled a driver to pick her up at the airport yesterday, and the young man had taken her directly to the office. There had been business matters that she had put on hold due to her trip to Michigan last week. Although it had taken her longer than anticipated to get through the paperwork requested by the Bureau, Arden had done an outstanding job in organizing the proper forms and reports. It had been around two o'clock in the morning before she made it home, only to then leave for the federal prison by six o'clock this morning.

Her meeting with the warden hadn't gone according to plan, but she was confident in the outcome. It had been mid-afternoon by the time that she had made it back to the office. Arden had been waiting for her with Sylvie's new furry companion in tow. Brook was no longer left wondering how a two-and-a-half-pound bundle of energy could make one a puddle of sap.

Warm lips pressed against the sensitive curve of her neck. Normally, such contact would have taken her by surprise had she not caught the familiar woodsy scent with a hint of sage seconds before contact. Brook turned to find Graham standing behind her in one of his Italian cut suits and his favorite grey and blue tie.

"You look beautiful," Graham murmured as he guided her away from the hostess stand.

His dark eyes swept over her black cocktail dress with matching high heels before meeting her pensive gaze. She wasn't the type of woman who took the time to enjoy such social settings. Before him, she would indulge in the occasional need for gratification.

Yet here she was...because of him.

"You made it," Brook said softly as they came to a stop near the far wall. "I left you a few messages."

"I thought I would surprise you like you did me," Graham said with a warm smile. "It means a lot to me for you to be here."

The messages that Brook had left on his voicemail had also included her intent to visit the prison. Only he had been able to see beneath the surface. She hadn't expected anything less. One of the reasons that she was drawn to him was his honesty, as well as his patience.

Brook had returned home for him.

It was a constant struggle for her to maintain intimacy, let alone permit others to be in her life in such a...well, normal manner. She didn't celebrate her own birthday let alone some-one else's milestone. Such a conscious decision was based on many valid reasons, but she was gradually becoming aware that she had allowed Jacob to have the upper hand all these years.

The entrance of Graham's mother pulled Brook from her private moment of understanding. With a grace unlike any oth-er, Elizabeth Elliott made her way across the restaurant's foyer while raising both hands to embrace her son. Before too long, the woman turned her attention toward Brook.

"You look absolutely stunning, my dear." Elizabeth kissed Brook on both cheeks before pulling back and resting both hands over her heart. "How can I ever thank you for such a perfect gift?"

"Gift?"

"Brook wasn't sure that she would be able to join us this evening, so she left a present for me on the table in the foyer—an abstract painting by an up-and-coming artist who will almost certainly take the art world by storm over the coming years." Elizabeth's smile widened as she pressed her hands together once again, the small handle of her evening bag hooked over the crook of her arm. "I will cherish the gift, and you being here means the world to me."

The hostess caught their attention with a warm smile and an elegant gesture. Graham signaled for his mother to follow the young woman. Brook remained near him as they made their way into the main dining area. The other patrons were engrossed in private conversations while the waitstaff expertly maneuvered throughout the room, serving dishes that were artfully arranged on plates. The enticing aromas reminded Brook that she had neglected to eat all day.

"You continue to surprise me, Brooklyn Sloane."

The manner in which Graham had made such a statement had Brook grateful that she had made the decision to join him. They spent the next two hours engrossed in stimulating conversation and indulging in menu choices that clearly delighted Elizabeth throughout the evening. The raspberry mousse in honey tuiles was her favorite. By the time they were served coffee, Elizabeth was dabbing the corner of her eyes in sentiment over Graham's generous donation to George Washington University to provide an art scholarship for those in need.

He had done so to honor both his mother and daughter.

Kelsey's death and subsequent investigation were the sole reasons why S&E Investigations, Inc. had opened its doors. Brook had been able to give Graham some closure, though no one would ever be able to heal the wounds of losing an only child.

"Thank you both for such a lovely evening," Elizabeth announced as she gently rested her cloth napkin next to her empty coffee cup. She covered Brook's hand with her own. "Brooklyn, thank you again for joining us this evening. My son is no longer walking through life without purpose, and it is all due to you. My son's happiness is the greatest gift by far."

Elizabeth picked up her evening bag that she had placed to the left of her place setting and tucked the purse underneath her arm. She stood while waving dismissively toward Graham, who had been in the midst of standing to assist in pulling back her chair.

"Nonsense. I'm joining some friends for a few after-dinner drinks," Elizabeth said as she stood from the table. There was no denying the woman's elegance. "Seeing as Brooklyn is flying back to Michigan first thing in the morning, I'm sure the two of you could use some alone time."

It wasn't long before Elizabeth walked gracefully toward the restaurant's foyer. The relief that washed over Brook from the sight of two men discreetly placing their napkins on their plates and following the older woman out of the main dining area was immense.

"Not until after he draws his last breath," Graham said casually as he reached for the stainless steel carafe that the waiter had set on the table. He refilled both their mugs as if they were having a normal conversation, though she had caught the edge of his tone. She also didn't need him to expand on the identity of said subject. "If I thought you would allow a protection detail, I wouldn't have hesitated to make such arrangements."

Brook had known about Elizabeth's protection detail since the very beginning, but such precautionary measures hadn't been brought up in recent conversations. Witnessing such a safeguard in person relieved some of Brook's stress.

"I can—"

"Protect yourself, I know." Graham took a drink of his coffee while maintaining eye contact. The way his brown eyes darkened told her that he was about to change the subject. "When do you fly out tomorrow?"

Brook lifted her own mug to cover her smile, which she had found herself doing more and more lately when she was with him. She had mentioned to Theo last week that she had to stop by Graham's estate to pick up some of her favorite suits. She hadn't realized until that very moment just how entwined her life with Graham had become.

Surprisingly, warmth had infused her instead of the usual flood of panic.

"I'll be here long enough for you to make me chocolate chip pancakes," Brook replied as she set her mug on the table. She kept one hand wrapped around the heated porcelain, but she

slid her right hand into his. "I take it you're home for the remainder of the week?"

"A few weeks actually." Graham amended as he stroked his
thumb over the back of her hand. "I have a few meetings lined up
at Quantico. We also have that appointment with the accoun-
tants at the end of May."

Graham was her silent partner in S&E Investigations, Inc.
He only ever attended financial meetings, while leaving the
day-to-day operations to her. He had kept his promise from day
one.

"Is there any way that I can convince you to give the team
hazard pay?" Brook was only half-kidding. Graham tightened
his hold on her hand, prompting her to change the subject.
While every single person involved in her life understood the
risks, that didn't mean she was absolved of guilt. "You know who
should have hazard pay? The nurses at the prison. It took me
hours to convince the warden that Jacob should be kept in isolation. I remember when we were young. He had reactive airway
disease. I don't want to take any chances that his breathing could
become so impaired that he would require hospitalization."

"Has Jacob shown any symptoms?"

"No, but that could change at any moment if the warden
doesn't take my suggestion regarding isolation."

"Jacob doesn't interact with the general population." Graham
continued to stroke the back of her hand as he enjoyed the rest
of his coffee. He made a valid point, but he also understood the
different ways that Jacob could manipulate any given situation.
"The guards in that section also don't oversee the main part of
the prison."

"But those guards share break rooms," Brook pointed out as
she caught sight of a woman pressing both hands to her chest,
similar to how Elizabeth had done earlier this evening. Both
gestures had bothered Brook, though she couldn't pinpoint the
reason why. "All it takes is one of the guards to be contagious

without realizing he is sick. He would then escort Jacob through the halls to the outside for his one hour of daylight, and then the transfer of droplets would be complete. I spoke to the two nurses myself, and they both say the strain of influenza making the rounds is severe. There is no reason to give Jacob an opportunity to escape when it could be fully avoided."

"Agreed." Graham followed her line of sight. "Do you know her?"

"No." Brook frowned, unable to explain what was bothering her about the reactions of both women. "It's nothing."

"It's always something," Graham said with a laugh as he released her hand so that he could signal for the check. "While we wait, walk me through the case."

"There's actually nothing to say," Brook admitted before taking the last sip of her coffee. She set the mug on the table before expanding on the lack of information. "We've hit a dead end. We're going to need to start at the beginning."

"Which is where you usually begin." Graham reached into his suit jacket to pull out his wallet. "Why is this one different?"

"Mary Four." Brook waved her hand when Graham arched his brow. "The team numbered the Mary Janes to keep the files separate. Anyway, you already know that Mary Four posted a video online, which was the reason the FBI contacted us. If the unsub is targeting women named Mary Jane Reynolds across the state of Michigan, it stands to reason that he has already started his surveillance on her daily routine."

"That makes sense." Graham paused long enough to hand his credit card to the server. "Why change avenues now?"

"Mary Four posted her video without reason. She hasn't noticed anyone following her, no phone calls, and no new people in her life." Brook studied the woman at the table, wondering what it was about her mannerisms and that of Elizabeth earlier this evening that garnered interest. "As far as we know, the victims didn't know one another. Bit can't find one connection to tie the three women together, either. We're wasting manpower by basically giving all potential victims twenty-four-seven security."

"If the unsub spends time monitoring his victims' routines, wouldn't the units posted outside the targets' homes push out his timetable?" Graham's question had been one that Brook had been mulling over for quite some time. "I suppose such efforts give you time to find him."

Brook had witnessed such initiatives before, and such actions had driven the unsub to ground...never to be heard from again. Those killers had been forced to either change their signatures or discover another outlet to ease their thirst for sin.

She hadn't stopped monitoring the woman, and when she rested her hand on her chest once more in a conspicuous fashion, it was enough incentive for Brook to reach for her phone. She quickly accessed the software program and pulled up previous online videos that Mary Four had posted to her social media accounts.

Brook rested her fingers on the display of her phone, pinching and zooming until the image expanded. Mary Four tended to rest her hand on her chest when she spoke to the camera. She had done so in their first meeting, but not because she was being dramatic.

"Mary Four is the target." Brook hastily accessed her speed dial list. She continued to speak to Graham while attempting to get Theo on the other end of the line. "The unsub stabs his victims in the heart. Mary Three was the only one stabbed in the back, but his focus was still on her heart."

"Shouldn't you be enjoying a birthday celebration?" Theo said in greeting over what sounded like live music.

"Mary Four had some type of heart surgery," Brook announced softly as the server appeared with Graham's receipt. She stood and motioned that she would wait for him out in the lobby. "From the tint of the scar, I'm guessing maybe a year ago?

I don't know why such a surgery would trigger the unsub to want her dead, but Mary Four is his target. Touch base with Agent Tirelli and have him swap out the local uniform for a federal agent. I want someone by her side until further notice."

"Seeing as Mary Four is sitting behind me at a table at the Crestlake Bar & Grill, I'll make sure to remain nearby until arrangements are made," Theo replied as the live music seemed to become even louder than before. "How could we have missed that in the background check? Or hell, even in her social media posts."

"HIPAA changed the landscape years ago. Also, Mary Four didn't post much over twelve or thirteen years ago. It has only been in the past year that she started to post daily." By the time Brook had answered Theo's question, she had walked past the hostess stand and claimed a corner area for privacy. Even at this late hour, the restaurant was at full capacity. "We'll need confirmation, of course. It's difficult to make out in the videos, but there are times when the tip of her scar can be seen in the V of her blouse."

"And the only thing the victims have in common is that the unsub targeted their hearts." Theo must have shifted his position, because the bass level had diminished significantly. "It makes sense, especially since we know that Mary Two's husband was at the clinic the night his wife was murdered. We assumed it was to ensure that she was alone, but what if the unsub was searching for proof that Mary Two had heart surgery? If I recall correctly, Mary Two was a patient of another family doctor, so her husband's clinic wouldn't have had any of her records. I'll reach out to Bit and Sylvie. They can start compiling a list of those involved with the surgery, though given what we know, that won't matter. The unsub has no idea which Mary Jane Reynolds had the surgery."

If the unsub had been someone connected to Mary Four's surgery, there would have been no reason for other deaths.

Brook's theory was missing something vital, but at least the investigation was once again moving forward.

"Have Sylvie contact the families of the three victims," Brook advised as she spotted Graham making his way through the main dining room. His dark gaze met hers, but there was no judgment in his eyes. He understood her, just as she understood him. "We can subvert HIPAA with a warrant, but that could take additional time. I'd rather Bit not circumvent any firewalls, either. Sylvie can ascertain whether the victims had heart problems. There is a chance the surgery doesn't mean anything in the grand scheme of things. See if she can find a connection through cardiologists, specialists, pharmacies, or even alternative medicine facilities. Once we have the warrant signed by a federal judge, Bit can then run a deeper search."

"Copy that."

"Oh, and Theo? Thanks for the push."

Brook lowered her phone and disconnected the call, not bothering to listen for any reply. Theo would have understood the underlying meaning of her statement. Besides, she had gotten her point across—his advice had been impeccable. There was no need for further discussion when her time with Graham was limited to this evening.

"Are you heading back tonight?" Graham asked as he finally joined her.

"No."

Graham slowly smiled in response to her profound answer. She returned his smile and tilted her head in anticipation, accepting the warmth of his kiss. The soft brush of his lips over hers promised an unforgettable evening.

"I do believe I'm getting the hang of delegating tasks, General Elliott."

Chapter Thirteen

Brooklyn Sloane

May 2024

Thursday — 11:26 am

"I NEVER UNDERSTOOD THE appeal of incense."

Brook stepped through the white picket fence surrounding the front yard of Mary Jane Reynold's home. There wasn't a cloud in the sky, though another round of storms were set to hit in the coming days. A gentle breeze carried the fresh scent of cut grass, courtesy of an older gentleman a few houses down. Brook inhaled deeply to clear out her sinuses.

"Studies have shown that the aromas from incense raise serotonin in the brain," Theo offered up as he made sure the gate latched behind him.

"You've been spending too much time with Sylvie," Brook muttered wryly as she came to a stop on the sidewalk. She glanced toward the rental car where she had locked her purse in the trunk. Theo had parked behind her in the SUV, and both vehicles appeared secure. "Serotonin? I'd be more worried about the risk of lung cancer."

"Mary Jane is scared, as well she should be," Theo pointed out as he glanced up and down the suburban street. The press had given up after two days of staking out Mary Four's residence after another story had caught their interest. All it would take was one whiff of the investigation potentially taking another direction to grab their attention and presence. "Agent Tirelli sent one of his colleagues to the house, but the agent didn't arrive until after two o'clock in the morning. Let's just say that by the time Agent Laurel made an appearance, every room in the house had its own incense. Wait. Cancer? From incense? Did you read that somewhere?"

"I take it back," Brook said as she scanned the houses across the street. "You've been spending too much time with Bit."

Bit and Sylvie had remained at the rental house. Between the two of them, they would be able to gather enough information regarding Mary Four's surgery to put together a long list of people to interview. Once they had those names in hand, Sylvie and Theo would be able to drive to Ann Arbor. They would handle the interviews, while Brook and Bit stayed in Crestlake.

Mary Four was the unsub's next target, which meant the un-sub was nearby.

"If I spotted the scar on Mary Four's chest during that online video, then the unsub would have noticed it, too." Brook noticed toys in one of the yards, which meant the woman who was giving an interview last week probably resided in that home. "A heart transplant? That opens the door for a long list of suspects."

Brook had spent the past hour convincing Mary Jane not to post a video about this new information, as well as how important it was for her not to change her daily routine. They stood a better chance at apprehending the unsub if he believed there was an opportunity he could reach her. While a federal agent had been appointed to safeguard Mary Jane, the unsub would assume the FBI would eventually tire and send him on his way. In the meantime, it was probable that the unsub would remain in the area to observe Mary Four's daily routine.

"Sylvie has been working on the paperwork to submit warrants for Mary Four's medical records, as well as everything related to her operation. And you're right about the net widening. We'll need to look into everyone involved in the transplant...the donor, the donor's family and friends, the recipients who were denied organs, and even hospital personnel who might have held a grudge from being denied involvement or some other far-out theory that caused the unsub to snap."

"Which means that we were right about this not being a typical investigation." Brook needed to adjust the profile now that new information had come to light. The individual who they were searching for was someone who had a specific target in mind. Given the collateral damage, the unsub wouldn't stop until he had completed his mission. "Listen, I didn't have a chance to eat breakfast. I'll stop and pick up lunch for everyone. Bit has already texted me twice to see if one of us is bringing back food."

"I'll meet you back at the house then," Theo said as he continued to monitor their surroundings. "I'm going to canvass the neighborhood. This street, anyway. We've had someone sitting outside Mary Four's residence for the past week. She hasn't been alone since posting her video, which could potentially force the unsub to find alternative means to study her routine."

Mary Four had agreed to allow Agent Laurel to remain inside her residence as of earlier this morning. As Theo had pointed out, a patrol car had been parked on the street. There could have been several ways that the unsub had attempted to garner information on his target. He could have posed as a law enforcement officer, asking questions about Mary Jane Reynolds. Then there were the traditional methods of gaining access and information, such as a handyman or a landscaper.

"I'll take the houses on the right."

"The kids are probably starving, M—"

"You can stop right there, Theo," Brook warned good-naturedly as she fastened the sole button on her blazer. The dark grey material soaked up the warmth of the sun, not that she would complain about it. While the day was what some would call perfection in terms of weather, the gentle breeze still held a crisp coolness that lacked humidity. "We'll work our way down and meet at the house across the way."

Theo's laughter from her previous warning carried in the air as she began to cross the street. She glanced back at Mary Four's residence, gauging how far the unsub might have attempted to gain information about his target. While everyone probably had superficial knowledge about those living inside the community, only those closest to each other would have the information that he would be seeking in this scenario.

Brook paused when she reached the third house across the street, pulling her credentials from her pocket. The suburban homes all seemed to blend together with their neat lawns and similar two-story architecture, but upon closer inspection, each one had its unique characteristics. Some had brightly painted doors, while others chose to stand apart with wooden porch swings or uniquely shaped shutters. The small difference gave each home its own personality.

It didn't take Brook long to walk up the two porch steps and knock on the screen door. She glanced to her left, noticing that Theo was already speaking to the older gentleman who had been mowing his grass.

"May I help you?"

"Good afternoon," Brook said as she held up her credentials. The older woman remained just inside the screen door as she tilted her head so she could look at the identification through her reading glasses. "My name is Brooklyn Sloane. My team and I are consultants with the FBI, and I was hoping to ask you a few questions."

"Is this about Mary Jane? I told my husband that her posting online all the time would lead to trouble," the older woman said as she pushed open the door. Her glasses had a thin chain attached to each temple tip, so they fell against her chest. "I'm Ruth. Ruth Pace. My husband's name is Charles."

She stepped out onto the porch, her seeking gaze finally landing on Mary Four's white picket fence. Ruth's voice contained a rasp that only belonged to smokers, but it was the yellowish tint on her index and middle fingers that confirmed the woman's habit.

"Have you noticed anything unusual in the neighborhood? People who don't belong? Suspicious vehicles?"

"Just the patrol car that has been sitting outside Mary Jane's house since last week." Ruth's eyes narrowed as she noticed said vehicle missing from its usual spot. "Have you made an arrest? Wait. No, you haven't, otherwise you wouldn't be here asking me questions."

Ruth was sharp, which meant that she didn't miss much that happened inside her community. Her observation came from smoking on the front porch, evident by the pack of cigarettes that were tucked discreetly against the windowsill near the porch swing.

"Just to clarify, no one has been knocking on doors in the past week? Maybe trying to sell something to you or asking if you have any yardwork for them to do?"

"No," Ruth replied as she gestured in the direction of Theo, who had already moved on from speaking with the gentleman who had been mowing his lawn. "We pretty much tend to our own yard, though Nathan mows a few of them."

"Nathan?"

"Laura's boy." Ruth nodded in the other direction. "Nathan is fifteen and has his driver's permit. He's saving up for his first car. He mows Mary Jane's yard. Maybe he would know, but you're out of luck today. Nathan and some of his friends went to the lake for the day."

"And the other neighbors? Anything out of the ordinary?"

"Not really," Ruth said as she shifted her stance to gesture toward her next-door neighbor. "You'll have to knock loud if you want Benji—Benji Torrence—to hear you over his television. He has hearing aids, but he never wears them."

Ruth frowned when she glanced past Benji's house.

"I haven't seen Janice in a couple of days, but you'll probably find her in the backyard. Morris is her last name. She can get a bit obsessive over her flower gardens."

Once again, Ruth had proven to be an invaluable source of information and insight.

"I appreciate your time, Mrs. Pace," Brook finally said after Ruth had practically gone through every neighbor within walking distance. By the time Brook had retraced her steps to the residence next to Ruth's house, Theo had finished speaking to those residing on Mary Jane's side of the street. Brook focused on the loud voices drifting through the open windows of Benji Torrence's house. She knocked hard on Ruth's advice. "Mr. Torrence?"

Brook figured if the older gentleman couldn't hear the low thud of her knocking, he might be able to pick up on her voice. She walked over to the screen inside the window and called out his name once more.

"I'm coming!"

Brook spent the next few minutes speaking with Mr. Torrence, but he wasn't as insightful into the community as Ruth. By the time Brook had walked up the porch steps of the house directly across from Mary Jane's residence, Theo was already next door speaking with another neighbor.

When Janice Morris didn't answer her door, Brook eventually made her way back down the porch steps. She carefully crossed the yard, mindful of her small heels. Vibrant flowers in various shades of pink and purple had been planted alongside the house. Among the blooms were stone butterflies of all shapes and sizes, which added a touch of charm to the two-story home.

Brook came to a stop at the edge of a wooden fence. She walked some of its length until she had a complete view of the backyard. A vegetable garden had been planted on the far side, and large flower pots with red and white perennials had been strategically placed on each corner of a patio deck. A bag of soil lay open on the stone pavers, along with several gardening tools.

Janice couldn't have gone far, so Brook reached for the latch on the gate.

"Ms. Morris?"

Brook thought that maybe Janice had gone back inside the house for a moment, but her mind changed when she stepped closer to the bag of soil. The clumps that had spilled from the bag had been dried by the sun. It was obvious the contents hadn't been touched for a few days. There were many valid reasons as to why Janice Morris had left such items outside, but something was off about the situation.

Brook cautiously stepped around the bag of soil, mindful of the hand trowel and cultivator. There were no gardening gloves in sight. She approached the sliding glass doors, but the heavy drapes had been pulled shut. The weight of the curtains had caused a gap between the two sides of the material, giving Brook the ability to step to the left in order to allow some sunshine to peer through the panes.

The spacious kitchen was quiet and still.

The limited rays that seeped through the slit in the drapes glinted off the light countertops. A quick scan revealed a few dirty dishes cluttering the sink, but overall, the interior seemed tidy.

What could be seen of the kitchen table revealed a simple vase...with dead flowers.

Brook tensed as she began to inspect the interior more close-ly, starting with the floor. Right at the corner of the counter, a streak of reddish-brown could be seen on the tiles. The darker tint of the stain revealed that the blood had dried days ago.

Ever so slowly, Brook unfastened the button on her blazer. She drew her firearm from its holster as she stepped to the side of the sliding glass door. The shift in movement allowed her to catch sight of Theo coming around the side of the house. He hadn't entered through the gate, so he would be able to retrace his steps with ease. She raised a finger to her lips before motion-ing that he should cover the front. He nodded his understanding before reaching for his weapon.

Surprisingly, the sliding glass door offered little resistance when she applied some pressure on the handle with her elbow. It wasn't her intention to disturb evidence, but if there was the slightest chance that Janice Morris was alive, then Brook needed to gain entrance into the house. She stepped over the threshold as quietly as possible.

A metallic scent lingered heavily in the air.

Brook slowly advanced into the home, examining every inch of space she could along the way. Now that she was standing close to the countertop, blood splatter on the hard surface was visible...enough for Brook to know that Janice Morris was dead.

Mindful of the smear on the floor, Brook made sure to step to the side as she rounded the island. A chair was missing from the kitchen table, but that wasn't what had captured her attention. A large pool of blood dominated the space, with streaks that led into the other room. Brook cautiously followed the crimson trail while straining to hear the slightest sound emanating from other parts of the house.

Brook silently entered the living room, coming to a stop when her gaze landed on the body of a woman. Her throat gaped open from the deep slice of a knife, and her eyes stared unseeing toward the ceiling. Given that the metallic scent of blood was stronger than the decomposition, Brook estimated Janice Morris' time of death to be around forty-eight hours.

Brook noted the missing kitchen chair tucked up against the far window, which just so happened to be facing Mary Jane Reynolds' residence. Their unsub had found another way to observe his next victim, and the death of a neighbor was proof of the unsub's desperation. Not willing to make assumptions that Janice Morris' killer had vacated the premises, Brook cautiously made her way over to the front door.

Keeping her weapon trained on the staircase leading upstairs, Brook reached over with her left hand and turned the deadbolt. She made a mental note to let the forensics team know she had left her fingerprints on the latch. Taking a step to the side so Theo could enter the house, she waited until he was prepared to help her clear the home. They fell into step, searched each room, and eventually returned to the living room.

"I'll make the call," Theo murmured as Brook crouched beside the victim.

The onset of rigor mortis had begun, but Brook noticed the absence of a struggle. Had Janice invited her killer into the house? If so, such conduct would have suggested surprise—or trust—allowing the unsub to draw near enough to deliver the fatal slice.

Theo was still on the phone with Agent Tirelli, who would be the one to initiate the process of bringing the medical examiner and a forensics team to the crime scene. Brook stood and made her way back toward the kitchen. She came to a stop when she had views of both the sliding glass door through the kitchen and the chair placed near the living room window.

Brook snapped her fingers to garner Theo's attention.

The unsub had almost certainly left the sliding glass door unlocked so that he could come and go as he pleased, which meant that there was a chance he planned on coming back at some point in the near future. Her profile suggested otherwise. The unsub was too intelligent to overstay his welcome. He would have noticed right away that the neighbors noticed even the slightest disturbance in the community. Still, she couldn't risk not covering their bases.

"Tell Tirelli to keep this quiet," Brook directed after Theo pulled the phone away from his ear. "No radios, no sirens, and no cars. We'll sneak in the medical examiner and one forensic tech through the back door after dusk. There's a chance—a slim one—that the unsub plans to come back to the house."

CHAPTER FOURTEEN

Theo Neville

May 2024

Friday — 1:49 am

THE STILLNESS INSIDE JANICE Morris' residence was heavy. Almost suffocating, though neither Theo nor Special Agent Rick Tirelli made a move to turn on the ceiling fan. The faint odor of blood and decomposition still hung in the air, and the fan would only further spread the smell around the lower level of the house. The medical examiner and two forensic techs had processed the scene and removed the body after dusk through the back sliding glass door.

"I'm surprised that Sloane isn't here," Rick said, his silhouette framed by the doorway leading into the kitchen. He shifted his weight to lean against the archway, causing the material of his pants to rustle. The slight sound was amplified by the deep quiet. "Is she planning on joining us at some point?"

"No." Theo had moved a kitchen chair to the corner of the living room. His eyesight had adjusted to the dim illumination, though the moonlight streaming through the sheer curtains had aided such effort. The victim had opted for heavier drapes in the kitchen, but her choice of living room décor had been beneficial to the unsub. "Brook drove back to the rental house to work on the profile."

A dog could be heard barking in the distance, but neither radio that had been supplied by Tirelli to the other agents and officers had come to life. Their immediate surroundings were under surveillance by both local law enforcement and federal agents. Theo and Rick would be notified instantly should anyone attempt to approach Janice Morris' home.

"No offense, but I don't get the whole profiling thing. The odds are in every profiler's favor when they point to a Caucasian male with mommy issues."

Theo rested the back of his head against the wall. He had been a skeptic himself until he had the privilege of working with Brook in the field. His view on the topic had quickly changed upon witnessing the way she could gather evidence and transform what she discovered into a single personality trait of a killer. With each discovery, she was able to describe everything about the unsub but his name.

"Would you label our killer as charming and sociable?"

"Nothing surprises me anymore with these sick fucks," Rick muttered before smothering a yawn. "I deal mostly with counterterrorism cases. The shit we see on a daily basis makes me have little faith in humanity. I get what you're saying, but that's a fifty-fifty shot, isn't it?"

"We're searching for someone who has been able to take time off work without suspicion, which indicates the unsub has a white-collar job with the ability to work remotely. He observes his victims for weeks if not months. He spends time getting to know either the victims themselves or their friends and family members. The video that Mary Jane Reynolds posted brought the attention of the police, the FBI, and the press. The unsub looks at Janice Morris as nothing but collateral, but he was successful in monitoring the neighborhood for a couple of days. Long enough for us to know that he will be searching for another way to reach his target."

"DNA was retrieved from the previous crime scenes," Rick pointed out, as if such evidence could help them this evening. There hadn't been a match in the system. "With the new suspect list your team is gathering, you will have a pool of men to retrieve samples and eventually obtain a match."

"You've made up your mind, Tirelli." Theo didn't have to point out that they couldn't legally go around and collect every single male subject's DNA without a warrant. Tirelli was well aware of the law's limitations. "Either you'll gain more insight into Brook's methods of solving cases and attempt to incorporate them into your own, or you'll stick with your old procedures. No harm, no foul."

It had been obvious from the time that Tirelli had entered the residence that he was a talker. He would choose idle chitchat over silence every time. Theo had worked with different agents during his tenure with the Bureau, and each had their own quirks. He didn't mind one way or the other, but the way S&E Investigations went about apprehending their targets wasn't up for debate.

Theo stretched his right leg, the sharp creak of the wood beneath him complaining with the movement. Sunrise was still hours away.

"Wait. Back up a second," Rick said as he glanced Theo's way. Particles of dust floated around his face which was captured in one of the angled moonbeams breaking through the middle of the curtains. "Is that why Sloane isn't here? She doesn't believe the perp is coming back here?"

"No, she doesn't," Theo replied truthfully as he switched to stretching his left leg. It wasn't like his answer would change their plans for the rest of the night. "I'm inclined to agree with her. The unsub realized right away that the community was close-knit. Nothing happens here without someone noticing, and the unsub was unfortunate in his choice of so-called collateral. Janice Morris preferred to be outside. It wouldn't have been long before one of her neighbors came to check on her."

"Well, shit."

Tirelli finally moved from his position, which gave him a view of both the front and back entrances. He had not moved far, though. Theo could hear what sounded like one of the three remaining kitchen chairs being moved from the table. Sure enough, the man's silhouette reappeared as he settled back underneath the arch dividing the rooms.

"You ever miss it? Working for the FBI, I mean."

Though the two men were close in age, they had been at the academy at different times. Theo had never met Rick Tirelli before this investigation, but rumors traveled fast through the Bureau. All Tirelli would have to do was place a single call to the West Virginia field office, which was where Theo had been stationed fresh out of the academy.

"I won't deny it was an adjustment."

The radio crackled, causing both men to tense. An exchange was made, but it was due to one of the officers noticing a vehicle entering the neighborhood. A quick license plate check verified that the car belonged to a local fireman who lived one street over.

"That doesn't answer my question," Rick pointed out as he leaned back against the chair, stretching out both legs so that he could cross his ankles.

"No. I redefined what was normal." Theo touched the band of his eyepatch. "If the Bureau called me back tomorrow—which I know would never happen—I'd turn them down flat. I'm where I need to be, and I'm grateful that Brook never doubted my ability."

"The two of you are close then?"

Theo could read where this conversation was heading as if a passage in a book had been marked with a yellow highlighter.

"I consider her my best friend," Theo replied, not seeing a reason to lie. "Tread carefully, Tirelli."

"I'm curious, is all. Sloane gave that interview a few years ago regarding her brother, so it's not like her childhood is some big, dark secret."

"Brook's past gave her a special insight into what makes a killer tick. Skills one can't learn from textbooks or classroom lectures," Theo explained as he stood from his chair. "Jacob Walsh is currently in federal prison, and Brook has her own life. There's no ground to cover, as far as I'm concerned."

Theo used the wall to help stretch some of his back muscles. Tirelli seemed to understand Theo had given all the information he was going to disclose on the subject. It was best to stick to the case.

"Sylvie and I will be driving to Ann Arbor either tomorrow or the following day to start interviewing the hospital staff involved with Mary Jane Reynolds' transplant surgery," Theo advised the agent, who was technically serving as the firm's FBI liaison. He would be looped in on the next steps of the investigation, anyway. "Considering the unsub wasn't sure which Mary Jane Reynolds was the recipient of the donor's heart, the answers could lie with the donor."

Tirelli snorted in humor, the sound filling the empty space of the living room.

"Are you telling me that we're looking for the son of a heart donor? A man who is pissed off that his mom's ticker is keeping someone else alive? Tell me again how wrong I am about pro-files, Neville."

Theo shook his head at Tirelli's comment, not bothering to respond. Most of the cases that come through the doors of S&E Investigation were serial killers in the typical sense, not someone bent on revenge or with a deranged sense of right and wrong. People reacted in many different ways to death, and it wasn't a stretch to believe that someone emotionally unhinged had lost all sense of sanity to someone's heart beating for another.

A loved one?

A son, as Tirelli had suggested?

Either theory was a possibility, but the team would still stick to their approach.

Theo slipped his phone out of his pocket. He had already made sure the display was on the lowest setting so that no one outside the house would notice someone inside. Once a message to the team had been sent that Theo or Sylvie should speak with the donor's family while the other questioned those involved on the transplant team, Theo accessed the two text messages that had come through no more than ten minutes ago.

"Tirelli?"

"Yeah?"

"That son theory might not be too far off." Theo slid his phone into the back pocket of his khakis before dropping into the seat. It was going to be a long night. "Only that doesn't really help us, because the donor was a foster mother. We'll need to weed through every child who lived under her roof over the past thirty years."

CHAPTER FIFTEEN

Brooklyn Sloane

May 2024

Saturday — 8:21 am

BROOK SLID THE DOOR open so she could enter the lake house. She had spent the past half hour on the deck while speaking with Special Agent Tirelli. Given that their suspect list had multiplied over the past couple of days, it was imperative to have his assistance to help weed through the red tape. She understood that he had been eager to hand off the investigation at the start, but now that they were aware Mary Jane Reynolds was in fact the target of their unsub, the narrative had changed drastically.

The western sky was already gathering clouds, but the approaching storm wouldn't reach Crestlake until later this evening. The accompanying winds had gotten a head start, bringing with them a hint of humidity.

Brook secured the sliding glass door behind her before closing the distance to the counter. She set her empty mug in the sink, not bothering with a refill. She planned on spending some time at the coffee shop in town, anyway.

Brook made her way into the living room to find Bit on the phone with Zoey. The two were setting a date as to when Bit would meet Zoey's parents. The upcoming introduction had been the topic of an ongoing discussion that he had continued to put off. From the sound of his side of the conversation, he had accepted his fate.

"Gotta go," Bit muttered when he caught sight of Brook. He set his phone on the table. "Boss, we've confirmed the clinic's filing cabinets were rifled through, but since the doctor's office where Duncan Reynolds is employed is paperless and has everything stored online, the unsub wasn't able to access any information."

"You didn't have to cut your call short." Brook picked up her leather bag that had been next to the couch. She would take her tablet to work on while sitting across the street from the boutique. Since the rain wasn't supposed to move in until later this evening, the coffee shop should still have its outdoor seating available. "I'm driving into town. I want to observe Mary Jane Reynolds' surroundings. The unsub has been forced to switch locations to observe her."

"We have an agent inside the store with her, don't we?"

"We do," Brook confirmed as she made sure she tucked her charging cord into a side pocket. "Which is why I want to monitor the surrounding area. A table outside the café will provide me with a discreet vantage point. Assuming that the unsub has watched Mary Four's online videos, he would have noticed her scar. He no longer has to search for his target. He's found her. The question remains if he is willing to sacrifice himself to carry out his mission."

"You mean, there is a chance that the unsub will go kamikaze?"

Leave it to Bit to sum up the potential scenario in such a straightforward manner.

"The profile suggests that the unsub will attempt to achieve his goal in such a way that he can go back to his life while having a sense of accomplishment." Brook flipped the front of her leather bag over so that she could fasten the snap. "That will change with each passing day. His reason for making sure the donor's heart stops beating will become more pressing, and he will feel as if he is suffocating. Such an awareness will have him compelled to take action."

"And figuring out the unsub's reason will lead us to his identity."

"Exactly," Brook said as she hooked the leather strap over her shoulder. She had left her purse and keys over on the entryway table near the front door, but she didn't move from her position. She wasn't one to give advice, but there were times when she made exceptions. Now was one of those times. "Bit, Zoey's parents will love you. Do you know why?"

"Not a clue," Bit muttered as he sat back in his chair. His right knee started to jostle almost immediately. "You all say that because you know me. They don't, and all they're going to see is some computer geek with a long nose, pale skin, and greasy hair."

"If you thought any of that mattered, you would change your daily routine to include time in the sun. You would dress differently, and you would also cut your hair. You don't, because you are comfortable in your own skin." Brook hesitated, but she decided to forge ahead with a comparison so that Bit understood the significance of his choices. "I might have changed my name when I turned eighteen years of age, but I accepted long ago that I will always be known as the sister of a serial killer. It is okay to be who we are, Bit."

The fact that Bit's upper body stopped moving in time with his leg meant that he had stilled his movements to hear her out. His gaze was downcast, but she definitely had his full attention.

"This team? We love you for being the man who went to extreme lengths to ensure his sister was taken care of during her cancer treatments. The man who spent every waking second with his best friend when she was in the hospital. We respect you for your loyalty, and we admire your dedication to those in your life. All Zoey's parents want is for their daughter to be happy, and you have succeeded in that department. Be yourself, Bit. Doing so will give them the ability to see you the way Zoey sees you."

Bit finally met Brook's gaze. His smile widened, and she realized she might have gone overboard in her so-called motivational speech. With a slight roll of her eyes, she walked toward the entryway table.

"You're on your own for lunch." Brook made a mental note to leave the pep talks to Arden, Sylvie, or Theo. "I'll bring dinner back, though."

"I'll let you know if anything pops on the Ann Arbor interviews." Bit rolled closer to the table, though his smile was still in place. "Sylvie is taking the family angle, while Theo will speak with the hospital staff. By the way, Jacob is still in solitary. There are fewer cases of influenza, so it seems as if the worst has passed."

Brook slid the strap of her purse over the leather one of her tote bag before picking up the keys to the rental car. Theo and Sylvie had taken the SUV to Ann Arbor. Should Bit need to go anywhere, he had the tech van, though he would probably walk to the bar and grill for lunch. A niggling thought about the pier had her turning back before reaching for the doorknob.

"Have you checked the camera setup out back? Anyone of interest?"

"None who stood out, but I'm using a software program to compare the other patrons every time Mary Four eats dinner over there. No one fits the profile so far, but the application is logged for recognition sweeps."

"Sounds good," Brook said as she finally opened the door. "I'll bring us back dinner from town. Maybe Italian."

"Extra garlic bread," Bit called out before Brook stepped out and closed the door behind her.

The rising humidity wasn't too bad, and the light blazer she wore was perfect to sit outside at a café table in town. She scanned the quiet street, taking note of any subtle differences in her surroundings. As she pressed the button on the key fob, the chirp of her phone sounded from the side pocket of her purse. The lock disengaged with a soft click, and she pulled open the driver's side door, leaning in to deposit her purse and leather bag onto the passenger seat.

Brook retrieved her phone, answering the call as she stood and closed the car door. She kept ahold of the keys as she turned around and began to walk down the small driveway.

"Morning," Brook greeted softly as her lips curved in a small smile.

"Are you any closer to closing the case?" Graham asked with a tone she had come to recognize very well. "I would truly like a repeat of what transpired after dinner last Wednesday night."

"Let's just say we're getting close," Brook replied with a light laugh as she stepped onto the street. He truly was good for her damaged soul. "Mind if I call you back this evening to discuss those details in private?"

"I'll be waiting. Be safe, Brooklyn."

She lowered the phone, knowing that he would be the one to disconnect. Switching the device into her left hand, she casually unfastened the button on her blazer so she could access her weapon if needed.

Brook had noticed the dark green Honda parked across the street the moment that she had stepped out of the house. Considering that the team had delved into Adam Bouras' background as thoroughly as possible, she had also known he was the one sitting behind the steering wheel. By the time she was mere steps away, Adam had opened the driver's side door and stepped out of his car.

"Mr. Bouras," Brook said in a relatively flat tone devoid of any emotion. "What can I do for you this morning?"

CHAPTER SIXTEEN

Sylvie Deering

May 2024

Saturday — 11:54 am

SYLVIE ADJUSTED HER SUNGLASSES as she kept her focus on Sheila Wallace's residence. Wallace had been an organ donor, and her heart had been given to Mary Jane Reynolds. With the SUV's engine shut off, the sun's rays intensified the warmth radiating off the dark dashboard. Seeing as only one vehicle was parked in the driveway, Sylvie wasn't in a rush to approach the front door.

"So Bouras was just parked outside the lake house?" Sylvie asked as she began to observe the other homes in the neighborhood. It wouldn't be a bad idea to knock on some doors to ask questions about Sheila Wallace. "Sitting in his car, and waiting for one of you to walk outside? What was his reasoning?"

"Bouras claimed to be checking in on the case, hoping to ease Mary Jane's concerns. He says that she isn't sleeping at night and is constantly on edge." Bit's voice was a bit muffled by the wind. He had mentioned that he was walking from the lake house to the pier for lunch. "Even though Bouras has alibis, Boss isn't too keen on his excuse as to why he sought out our physical location."

"Which was...what?" Sylvie prodded as movement in her rearview mirror caught her attention. An older model car was slowly pulling to a stop behind her. "I need to go, Bit."

"Bouras claimed that he couldn't find Boss' business card that she left with Mary Jane at the house," Bit summed up quickly while Sylvie unfastened her seatbelt. She quickly removed her sunglasses. "Anyway, the reason that I was calling was to tell you that no one deleted Sheila Wallace's social media accounts. She had no social media presence to begin with...none."

"Thanks, Bit." Sylvie reached into one of the cup holders where she had stored her eyeglasses. She wiped away a smudge on the black rims before settling them on the bridge of her nose. "I'll let you know how the interviews go this afternoon. Bye."

Sylvie lowered her phone as she checked her side mirror. A man stepped out of the car, thus removing the glare from the front windshield. She recognized him from his picture—Tyler Doss. He was thirty years old, and he had been placed with Sheila Wallace at the age of sixteen years old. Sylvie and Bit had spent hours collecting names and photographs of every child placed in Sheila Wallace's home who would fit the age parameters of their unsub.

After collecting her purse and palming the keys, Sylvie reached for the door handle. The temperature was a tad cooler outside the SUV, and there was the faint scent of fresh-cut grass lingering in the air. She shut the door with a slight shove before offering her hand.

"Tyler Doss? I'm Sylvie Deering," she introduced before taking a step back. She had worn a light pink cardigan over a pair of white pants. She had paired with it a thick mauve belt to have a comfortable place to holster her weapon. The man's gaze immediately dropped to her firearm. "I appreciate you and the others meeting me here."

Tyler Doss was broad-shouldered, sported a beard, and wore an inexpensive suit that most car salesmen dressed in during the workday. His grip had been firm, but it was obvious from his frown that he would rather be anywhere else but Sheila Wallace's residence.

"You didn't say what this was about." Tyler fell into step beside Sylvie as she began to walk up the driveway. "Why is the FBI interested in Sheila Wallace? She died last year."

"There has been some information that has come to light over the past few days," Sylvie said, purposefully keeping her response vague. "I'm surprised that the house hasn't been listed for sale yet."

"Sheila didn't have any kids of her own, so she left it to Andrea." Tyler stepped forward quickly so that he could reach for the screen door. "Here. Let me get that."

Andrea Simpson was the woman who had inherited Sheila Wallace's home. While Andrea hadn't been the donor's biological daughter, their relationship must have been close enough to warrant a will. Such information could come in handy over the next few hours.

Sylvie nodded her appreciation to Tyler before stepping over the threshold. The house didn't have a porch, and it didn't appear as if Andrea had taken an interest in gardening. The flowerbeds contained dead leaves, and the only reason the soil appeared somewhat healthy was courtesy of the recent rains.

Sylvie caught the faint, stale odor of old cigarette smoke as she entered the living room. The smell lingered in the air, but any quick movement caused the scent to vanish. The musky aroma simply wasn't overpowering enough to assume that Andrea was the smoker.

Stepping into the living room was like entering the past—one wall consisted of wooden panels from the 70s, while the other three had faded wallpaper that peeled at the edges. The darkness of the room cast shadows everywhere, making it all too easy to notice the dust floating in the sunlight that streamed through the windows.

"Ty? Is that you?" A woman materialized from what Sylvie assumed was the kitchen. "Oh, you must be the FBI agent."

"Consultant," Sylvie corrected as she reached out to shake the woman's hand. "My name is Sylvie Deering, and I work with S&E Investigations out of Washington, D.C."

"Hey, Andrea." Tyler stepped around Sylvie so that he could kiss Andrea on the cheek. Sylvie didn't pick up anything more intimate than a brotherly and sisterly vibe. "It's been a while. Sorry about that. Business has been booming since the warm weather moved in."

Andrea patted Tyler's hand before gesturing that Sylvie should take a seat. The living room furniture hadn't been updated in decades. The blue and brown fabric of the couch and matching chairs were frayed in the front from overuse, and there were indentations in the cushions.

"Can I get you anything to drink? A water? Soda?" Andrea offered as she didn't follow behind Tyler and Sylvie right away. "I might have some apple juice, too."

"No, thank you," Sylvie replied as she claimed the chair. She set her purse on the floor. "I just have a few questions, but should we wait for Mitch Swilling?"

"Mitch?" Tyler's body language suggested disbelief upon hearing the man's name. "Andrea, you didn't tell me that Mitch was back in town."

"Then maybe you should come around more often." Andrea' sharp reply startled Sylvie. The woman had initially come across as quite timid. "Sorry. I'm a little stressed since I was let go from the hotel. Mitch came back into town around six months ago. He's been dropping in every now and then, so when the FBI called about Sheila, I told Mitch that he should be here."

Tyler cleared his throat when he realized that Sylvie was quietly waiting until they were done speaking to ask her questions. She wouldn't have minded if they had continued their conversation.

"I haven't seen Mitch in years," Tyler explained as he rested his elbows on his knees. He didn't bother leaning back against the cushion, and his body language suggested that he wasn't comfortable in the house. "As you already know, Sheila was our foster mother. There were a lot of foster kids in and out of this place."

"What can you tell me about Sheila?" Sylvie asked, deciding not to wait for Mitch. Tyler might be more inclined to answer questions without someone else around whom he clearly wasn't comfortable with. "Was she a good foster mother?"

Tyler's jaw clenched as he turned to stare at Andrea. Andrea slowly inhaled while giving Sylvie a tight smile. She certainly had her answer.

"Sheila was okay. She didn't go above and beyond, and she left us alone for the most part." Andrea subconsciously began to pick at her cuticles. "I've been in worse homes."

"We were walking, talking checks. It's that simple." Tyler's tone was flat. "When the first of the month came, we'd get a home-cooked meal. The rest of the time? We were on our own. Sheila gave us all one shelf...collectively. Sometimes there was food on it, other times it was bare."

Sylvie camouflaged her wince by glancing down at her wrist. She had gotten used to wearing a smartwatch to monitor her heart rate during her recovery, and she liked that the watch linked to her phone. The fact that Bit would be able to track her should something else just as tragic happen gave her a sense of security.

"Miss Simpson, is that how you—"

"Call me Andrea," she replied with a shrug.

"Andrea, is that how you recall what it was like to live here?" Sylvie inquired, curious as to why someone would opt to stay in a place with such appalling memories. "I'm aware that Sheila left you her home, but you could have opted to sell the house for cash."

"Knowing that I have a permanent place to live is worth more than what a realtor could get me for this place," Andrea said with an unmistakable bitterness. "Besides, Sheila treated the girls better than the boys. I actually didn't move out when I turned eighteen. I was on a cleaning crew at a local motel. I offered to pay rent, and Sheila took me up on it. I was one of the last fosters in this place anyway. Her health had started to take a turn for the worse."

"Was Sheila ever physically abusive to any of the foster children?"

"No."

Both Tyler and Andrea had spoken in unison, but it was clear that Sheila had done enough damage without needing to lift a hand. Sylvie began to warm up to the idea that their unsub might have been one of the children placed in Sheila's care.

"It's my understanding that Sheila had about thirty-six children in and out of her home over a span of fifteen years. Do you know if any of them would have wanted to hurt Sheila?"

"No," Tyler said a bit too hesitantly for Sylvie's liking, but she got the sense that he wasn't hiding information as much as he was thinking back to his childhood. "As Andrea said, we were the last batch of kids to be placed here before Sheila's health started to decline. She—"

"...was a cold-hearted bitch."

A deep voice came through the screen door before it swung open and revealed a tall, lean man whom Sylvie recognized as Mitch Swilling. The picture that Bit had uploaded to their files must have been from a time when the man had an affinity for facial hair. He was currently clean-shaven, and his thin lips were compressed in disgust.

"Mitch," Tyler greeted in a rather deadpan tone. It was obvious that the two men didn't get along. "It's been a while."

"Years, but who's counting?" Mitch had yet to take his gaze off Sylvie, but it had nothing to do with her looks and everything to do with her reason for requesting to speak with them. "You the fed?"

"Consultant." Sylvie stood from the chair, her movements deliberate. She shook his hand, determined not to display any emotion when he tightened his grip more firmly than needed. "I appreciate you taking time off work to speak with me, Mr. Swilling."

Sylvie had purposely phrased her statement in such a way as to prompt a typical person's reply, which would normally contain detailed information. Considering that Bit hadn't been able to ascertain an employer for Mitch, she was interested as to how the man made his living.

Unfortunately, Mitch didn't take the bait.

"Why are you here asking questions about Sheila?"

Sylvie reclaimed her seat, not letting on that Mitch's decision to remain standing unsettled her. It was clear that had been his intention, but she had learned from the best not to wear her emotions on her sleeve.

"I've got to say that I'm a bit curious about this line of questioning, too," Tyler said after he let his gaze slide away from Mitch in disgust. Depending on how long Theo wanted to remain in Ann Arbor, Sylvie would suggest speaking with each of these people on an individual basis. They were liable to garner more information that way. "You asked if we knew of anyone who wanted to hurt Sheila, but it wasn't like she was murdered last year. She had a stroke."

"We have it on good authority that a donor recipient's life is in danger, and we believe that the imminent threat is in connection to the transplant operation," Sylvie replied without giving away too many pertinent details. "We're merely touching base with anyone associated with the donor, the recipient, and those individuals involved in the operation."

"Are you saying that she was murdered?" Andrea asked in confusion.

"No, I'm not saying anything of the sort. There are just some details that we need to confirm regarding her status as an organ donor."

Tyler's hand found the back of his neck once more. He didn't handle stress well, and she figured that he popped antacids daily. Working on commission probably didn't help his anxiety level, either. Mitch, on the other hand, didn't react to her response one way or the other.

"You mentioned that the three of you were the last of the foster children placed in Sheila's home, but did you ever meet any of the previous foster kids? Maybe someone who harbored resentment toward her?"

"We all resented her." Mitch didn't mince his words. "The foster system is broken, and by the time the kids reach their teens, they know the difference between a bad placement and one that can get them through until the age of eighteen. This place was the latter. Doesn't mean it was all peaches and cream. You still haven't answered our questions."

"And your social worker?" Sylvie asked, refusing to allow her emotions to enter her voice. "I believe his name is Fred Dawkins. Was he aware that Sheila wasn't the model foster mother? Did anyone inform him that Sheila was ignoring her responsibilities?"

Mitch began to laugh, but he let it fade when Andrea shot him a sideways glance of annoyance. She crossed her legs and slipped her hands in between them as she answered Sylvie's questions.

"Mr. Dawkins went above and beyond in his duties as a social worker. He was always there, always willing to meet us if we needed him." Andrea gave a small smile as she recounted a few memories. "He would meet us at the youth center and play basketball with those who wanted a game or just sit on the bleachers and talk to us."

"Look, Dawkins knew that Sheila wasn't the best placement, but the choices were slim back then. I'm assuming they still are," Tyler said as he finally lowered his hands. "I wouldn't want that man's job, and I get why he checks on the kids often. If anything goes sideways, he is the one who would shoulder that responsibility."

Fred Dawkins didn't fit the profile, but that didn't mean he wouldn't have an idea as to who might harbor such deep-seated hatred toward Sheila Wallace that all sense of right and wrong had gone out the window. Sylvie had a meeting scheduled with him later this afternoon.

"And your thoughts on Fred Dawkins?" Sylvie asked Mitch after she had caught the slight shake of his head.

"I have none. Are we done here? I have somewhere to be, and it is obvious that you're not going to share the real reason you're here."

"Thank you for your time," Sylvie said, reaching for her purse. She pulled out three business cards. "Here is my contact information. If you happen to think of anything in the coming days regarding our conversation, I would appreciate a call."

Sylvie sensed that Mitch wasn't going to move out of her way, so she gracefully stepped around him. The screen door would have clattered shut behind her if she hadn't kept ahold of the handle. There were low murmurs of conversation drifting through the screen after her departure, but she couldn't make out what was being said between the three of them.

Sylvie had made it halfway down the drive before Tyler's voice brought her to a stop. She turned and waited patiently for him to reach her.

"Dawkins has a son around our age. I haven't seen either of them in years, but Shane used to come to the youth center with his dad every now and then." Tyler smoothed his tie before buttoning his jacket in such a manner that it was almost as if he were uncomfortable with providing her with such information. "Shane used to say that if he were in our position, he'd kill her. Sheila, that is. It's not my intention to get anyone in trouble or on the radar with the feds, but I thought you should know."

"Thank you, Mr. Doss." Sylvie didn't turn around quite yet. She got the distinct impression that Tyler had waited until they were alone to part with his opinion on Fred Dawkins' son. "Why share this with me now?"

The screen door suddenly opened, and Mitch came strolling out, his eyes narrowing at the sight of Tyler and Sylvie still standing in the driveway. They were far enough away not to have their private conversation overheard, which was probably the only reason that Tyler answered her question.

"Mitch and Shane were friends...probably still are," Tyler murmured as he began to walk down the driveway. "I left my old life behind as much as possible, Miss Deering. I'd like it to stay that way."

CHAPTER SEVENTEEN

Theo Neville

May 2024

Saturday — 3:21 pm

THEO WAS GRATEFUL THAT Lucy Burrow, who held the Chief of Staff position at the hospital where Sheila Wallace had been taken off life support, had granted him permission to use one of the conference rooms on the top floor. Not even the distance between levels could lessen the potency of the antiseptic scent that made him nauseous. The strong odor brought back memories that he would soon rather forget.

"I'm about to meet with Fred Dawkins," Sylvie informed Theo, her face close to the screen of her phone as she shut the door to the SUV. Her black-rimmed glasses were slightly askew, but she fixed them before walking across what appeared to be a small parking lot. "Bit wasn't able to find much on the man's son. Shane basically fell out of sight after high school. I don't think Tyler had the right information regarding Mitch's friendship with the man. I think we might need to spend the night, because it would be near impossible to speak to everyone on our list by tomorrow morning."

"Arden took the liberty of making us reservations at a Marriott for the next two nights," Theo advised her, picking up his empty coffee mug. The white porcelain had the hospital's logo on the side, but he didn't like the shape of the rim. The contents tended to roll over onto the table, causing him to constantly use a napkin to wipe away the drips. "When he saw how many names were on the hospital staff who were included in the transplant operation, he booked the closest hotel to the hospital."

Theo closed the distance to a long table in the back of the conference room that basically served as a beverage bar. Lucy had one of her staff bring in a tray of sandwiches and fruit, though Theo hadn't touched any of the food. He held his mug underneath the spout of a coffee dispenser and pressed the pump several times. He couldn't help but inhale deeply, but the delectable aroma failed to mask the hospital's clinical smell.

"I miss my ginger lemon tea," Sylvie muttered as she continued to walk, jarring the phone up and down with each step. "Once I finish speaking with Dawkins, I'll head your way. I haven't had a thing to eat since we left Crestlake, so I suggest an early dinner."

"I'll be waiting by the front doors in about an hour."

Theo retraced his steps after ending the video call to set his phone on the table. He glanced at the large black and white clock on the far wall, noting that Kevin Volson was now over a half hour late. Considering the nurse's schedule, Theo understood that he had to be flexible, which was why he had spent the past thirty minutes combing through the notes that he had jotted down from his previous interviews.

A lot of personnel had been involved with the transplant operation. Between the donor and recipients, there were attending physicians, anesthesiologists, an organ harvesting team, surgeons, perfusionists, scrub nurses, ICU nurses, and a slew of other positions needed to carry out such delicate surgeries. Theo hadn't gotten through half the people on his list, but Kevin Volson had been Sheila Wallace's floor nurse when she had first been admitted to the hospital.

Theo made himself comfortable in one of the rolling chairs at the end of the large table. He jotted down a note to request from Lucy a list of administrative personnel who also might have had access to the organ recipients. Once he clicked his pen and set down the small notebook that he always carried with him when in the field, Theo picked up Volson's personnel file.

Kevin Volson was twenty-nine years of age and an Ann Arbor native with an unblemished record. The picture taken for his identification badge displayed a short hairstyle, a round face, and a scar through his left eyebrow.

A knock garnered Theo's attention, and he glanced up as the conference door opened to reveal his next interviewee. Theo motioned for Volson to enter before closing the manilla folder.

"Mr. Neville? I am so sorry to keep you waiting." Kevin pushed the door open with his shoulder wide enough so he could carry in a tray with a plate of food and a beverage. "We had two new admissions, and it took longer than we thought to get things squared away. Dr. Burrow said that you wouldn't mind if I ate my lunch during our meeting."

Considering that it was after three in the afternoon, Theo could only imagine that the man's stomach had shrunk, especially given that his shift had started at six o'clock this morning. The delicious smell of lasagna was better than the antiseptic odor anyway.

"I don't mind at all," Theo said as he gestured toward the table. Once Kevin had placed his tray opposite of Theo's seat, the two men shook hands. "I appreciate you taking time out of your day to speak with me. I know you only have a few minutes, so I'll be as brief as possible."

"Suzie is covering for me, so I'm good for the next thirty minutes or so." Kevin took a seat before picking up his fork. The fact that he didn't blow on his food while there was steam rising from the plate suggested that he often wolfed down his meals. "Dr. Burrow said this is in regard to an organ donor patient from a year ago?"

"Yes, Sheila Wallace." Theo wasn't one to carry a briefcase, but he had brought with him the tablet that he normally used when in the office or at home. He slid the device over, ensuring that Sheila's picture stayed on the screen. "Do you remember her?"

"Yes," Kevin replied after swallowing a rather large bite. He paused to take a drink of what appeared to be apple juice. That wouldn't have been the beverage Theo would have chosen to go with an Italian dish, but to each his own. "Hard to forget, since someone missed the fact that Wallace had a DNR. She never should have been placed on life support."

Theo had been well-versed in Sheila's care during the days before her organs had been harvested. Dr. Burrow had taken time to explain that Sheila had suffered a stroke, but someone on the staff missed the DNR on file. Sheila had been placed on life support, and the oversight had posed a problem for all involved. It had been around that time when Andrea Simpson had discovered that Sheila had appointed her power of attorney.

Since Theo and Sylvie were staying overnight in Ann Arbor, they would need to make time to speak with Andrea Simpson again. It was imperative to find out if anyone had attempted to talk her out of following Sheila's wishes as an organ donor. Theo or Sylvie could have simply called Andrea, but Sylvie mentioned that it would probably be best to go back in person when Doss and Swilling weren't present.

"Is that what this is all about? Did the daughter decide to file a lawsuit?"

"No, nothing like that," Theo replied as he reached for his tablet. He switched screens so that Andrea Simpson's photo was front and center. "Is this the daughter you are referring to?"

"Yes." Kevin took another bite as his attention switched from the screen to Theo. "Her brother was there, too."

Theo switched out the picture for one of Tyler Doss.

Kevin nodded his recognition while chewing the remainder of his food. He reached for his napkin, wiping his lips before giving more insight into Andrea and Tyler's relationship. It was obvious that the two hadn't clarified their affiliation with Sheila.

"I felt for them. I really did, because I don't know if I would have handled the situation as well as they had after discovering the error."

"Do you recall anyone else visiting Sheila Wallace?"

"No, but the patient was here for close to three days before the organ transplant team took over." Kevin paused eating long enough to take another drink of his apple juice. He screwed the cap back on before setting the bottle on the tray. "I'm sure Dr. Burrow has a list of the other nurses who were in charge of Ms. Wallace's care. They might have had conversations with other family members."

"Did you happen to see this man?" Theo reached out and swiped to the right so that Fred Dawkins' image appeared on the screen. "Or this man?"

Kevin pushed his tray to the side as he leaned in close to inspect Shane Dawkins' photograph.

"I went to high school with that guy."

Given that the photograph Bit had uploaded to the software program was one from at least six or seven years ago, it was no wonder that Kevin would refer to Shane as a kid. The two were close in age, but Theo had never expected there to be such a connection between the two.

"His name?" Theo wanted confirmation. "And did you see him at any time at the hospital during the period of Sheila Wallace's admission?"

"Shane Dawkins." Kevin took the liberty of scrolling backward. "Yeah, that is definitely Mr. Dawkins. Our high school had close to a thousand students, so it wasn't like we hung out together. But I do remember Shane from back then. And to answer your question, no. I haven't seen either of them for over ten years. What do the Dawkins have to do with Sheila Wallace?"

"Fred Dawkins is a social worker, and Sheila Wallace was a foster parent many years ago. We're investigating anyone who might have had a grudge against Ms. Wallace."

"Wallace suffered a stroke, though," Kevin replied with a frown. He leaned forward until he could rest his arms on the table, the tray moving with the motion. "I was her nurse, and I read over her chart thoroughly."

Theo continued on with the interview, averting the need to share the real reason behind his questions. The mere mention that a recipient's life was in danger would spark a full-blown panic that the Bureau and S&E Investigations didn't need at the moment. Twenty minutes later, Theo brought their meeting to an end.

"Kevin, before you go," Theo said as he stood while observing the nurse pick up his tray. "Did you ever overhear anyone on the organ transplant team talk about any of the recipients?"

"No, but my involvement ended when the team took over." Kevin held the food tray in one hand. "They handle everything from that point on."

"Thank you, Kevin. You've been very helpful."

Kevin stepped to the side before pushing his chair back underneath the table. After exiting the conference room, Theo motioned to him that the door could be left open. A security camera could be seen in the hallway, and the sight of it prompted Theo to check on the warrant that he had submitted earlier for footage of the hospital. The response from the judge wasn't exactly what he had hoped for, but it would have to do for now.

Theo picked up his phone and accessed his speed dial.

"Bit, it's Theo. We were only granted access to the security footage on Sheila Wallace's floor, and there was also a time span given—from the moment of admission to when her remains were taken to the funeral home." Theo had initially requested access to all the hospital's security footage, but judges were leery about too much leeway being given due to the intricate language of the HIPAA laws. "If our unsub was in the hospital at any point during the time Sheila Wallace was on life support, let's hope that he was able to access her floor so that we have something concrete to go on."

"There could be a way around that, Big T."

Bit's voice became clearer when he turned down the volume of his music. The fact that he was blaring anything other than light jazz told Theo that Brook had yet to return to the lake house for the day.

"No," Theo stated matter-of-factly. "We stick to the rules this time around."

Theo wasn't proud of the lengths that he had gone to a few months ago after Sylvie had been attacked and Brook had basically been abducted and taken hostage. Theo had crossed lines that his parents never would have during their careers. While he was still coming to terms with his previous decisions, he didn't regret doing what was necessary to pinpoint Brook's location at the time.

"'O ye, of little faith," Bit exclaimed before correcting Theo's assumption. "What I meant to say was that if I can prove that someone is just out of frame on the security footage, preventing us from identifying said person on Wallace's floor, then we can put in for another warrant on the grounds that we need access to some of the entrances from other angles."

"Just for that potential workaround, I'll buy you a jumbo bag of Skittles on our drive back to Crestlake," Theo said right as Dr. Burrow appeared in the doorway. She held a blue folder in her hand, which he was sure would include the names of the administrative personnel who had access to the list of donor recipients. While Theo had been vague with those he spoke to about his reasoning for such probing questions, he had been truthful with Dr. Burrow. "I'll touch base with you later tonight."

Theo disconnected the line while studying Dr. Burrow's features. The thin, vertical lines above her upper lip deepened as she frowned in what appeared to be disappointment. Maybe frustration, but he was about to find out which one as he set his phone on the table.

"Mr. Neville, I don't know if this helps your investigation, but it's come to my attention that Sheila Wallace's heart was initially meant to go to another patient," Dr. Burrow advised after she stepped into the conference room and closed the door quietly behind her. She stepped forward and handed over the folder. "The only reason the heart was not flown to the recipient at the top of the list was due to inclement weather. Every effort was made, but in the end, it was decided that Mary Jane Reynolds should receive the organ due to her proximity and the fact that she was second on the list."

"Thank you, Dr. Burrow."

Theo spent a few minutes discussing with her the best approach to speaking with the administrative personnel, and they both agreed that she should take the rest of the evening to set up the interviews to begin tomorrow morning at seven o'clock sharp. Once he was left alone to gather his belongings, he tucked the phone on his shoulder as he waited for Brook to pick up his call.

"We have a problem, Brook. There was a thirty-three-year-old man by the name of Reggie Hollins who was supposed to receive Sheila Wallace's heart. He has since died, and his family is now suing the hospital. I'll spare you the details for now, but suffice it to say the heart went to Mary Jane Reynolds instead. We're going to need Tirelli's help to weed through all the interviews. Our suspect pool has now turned into a damned lake."

CHAPTER EIGHTEEN

Bobby "Bit" Nowacki

May 2024

Saturday — 7:48 pm

THE RELENTLESS RAIN BEAT against the glass panes of the bar with such ferocity that it was obvious something had upset Mother Nature. Every flash of lightning illuminated the outside world through the windows to display leaden drops slamming against the hoods of parked vehicles and the asphalt below before plunging the chaotic scene back into darkness. Thunder rolled in the distance, but it was a dull roar compared to the laughter, clinking glasses, and the pulsating beat of music inside the bar.

The heavy bass reverberated through the wooden floorboards and up into Bit's chair. He always wondered if such vibrations altered the rhythms of people's heartbeats. He rubbed his chest at the thought of having a heart attack so young.

Brook had claimed a chair to his left at a table in the back of the bar. The original plan of her bringing dinner back to the lake house had been altered by the storm front. Mary Jane Reynolds and her fiancé had decided to stay in town and join friends for some drinks at a local bar. The Crestlake Bar & Grill had closed down for the night due to the inclement weather, so their usual hangout hadn't been an option.

The group was at a nearby table, where Mary Jane laughed as her friend leaned in to share something private. Adam's arm rested on the back of her chair. Unless one had firsthand knowledge that a killer wanted her dead, no one would ever be the wiser.

"We don't really do things like this one-on-one, huh?" Bit said as he attempted to find a topic unrelated to the case. He glanced her way, wondering if she would rather discuss the investigation. Just in case, he quickly spoke so that Brook didn't have to comment on his previous question. "I thought a federal agent was supposed to be with Mary Jane twenty-four-seven."

Brook gave a discreet nod toward the far end of the bar. A man occupied one of the three stools, though the dim lighting obscured his features. The baseball cap helped with that endeavor, as well. He remained inconspicuous, nursing a drink with an easy indifference that belied his true purpose.

"He's good." Bit reached for a shelled peanut before squeezing it with his fingers. Once it broke apart, he picked out the two nuts. "Hey, you don't think our unsub has police training, do you?"

Brook shook her head, her long black hair moving slightly up and down as the strands rested over her left shoulder. It always amazed him that she had features that were so different than those of her brother. Whereas Jacob's jawline was square like his father's, Brook took after her mother. Her heart-shaped face with high cheekbones made for a beautiful combination. Not that Bit thought of her as anything other than his boss and friend.

"No. Our unsub has had too many missteps. I'm convinced he works remotely, which gives him the flexibility to stalk his victims at will. Plus, his DNA isn't in the system." Her gaze never actually landed on Mary Jane, but Bit figured Brook wasn't missing a single action that took place at the woman's table. "He didn't have to work that hard with Mary Four, did he?"

As if on cue, Mary Jane raised her phone, capturing the pink hues of the beverage inside her glass. With precision, she made a few swipes on her phone before setting it down and rejoining the conversation. Bit's phone vibrated almost immediately against the wooden tabletop. He glanced at the screen, noting the social media alert. Mary Jane's post was already gathering momentum online...but her location had been turned off. At least she had taken some of Brook's advice.

"I had a long conversation with Mary Jane today during her break." Brook reached for her club soda. She took a sip before meeting Bit's gaze. "We came to an understanding. At first glance, Mary Jane appears to be enjoying herself. She is laughing with her friends, reaching out and casually touching her fiancé's knee, and even joining in on the conversation as if nothing was wrong. Look closer. Her gaze darts to the door every time someone enters the bar. When she reaches for Adam's knee, it's usually when someone walks by their table. And her drink? She's nursing it, which is why she was able to take a picture ten minutes after it was delivered to her table."

"Why even post to social media then?" Bit asked in confusion, reaching for another peanut. "I mean, she has gotten hundreds of reactions in seconds. She'll have thousands within minutes. Also, everyone in the comments is asking for an update on the case."

"On one hand, Mary Jane has to keep her daily routine the same. She can't put her life on hold. That doesn't help her, and it certainly doesn't help us." Brook set her drink on its designated napkin. "I did request that she omit the location tags on her posts. It's one thing to maintain a day-to-day schedule, but there is a fine line between being in danger and taunting the man who wants to take her life."

Bit was prevented from continuing the topic of discussion when a waitress came toward them with a tray of food. Granted, it was bar food, but he wouldn't complain. Just the sight of a greasy burger and fries had his stomach rumbling louder than the thunder. Or the bass. He wasn't sure which was louder at this point.

"Mary Jane wanted to go straight home after work," Brook said as she spread a thin paper napkin over her lap. She had ordered boneless teriyaki chicken wings and a basket of fries. Normally, she would have requested traditional wings. The way she casually kept examining their surroundings had him realizing that she wanted to be free to draw her weapon with ease should something unforeseen take place. "It was Bouras who talked her into staying out tonight."

"Are you saying—"

"No, I don't believe the unsub is working with someone." Brook used her fork to divide one of the wings into smaller bites. "I spoke with Agent Tirelli, and he has interviews lined up with Reggie Hollins' family members. The scope of this investigation is wide. By the way, you've done an excellent job merging the information. I know it isn't easy with intel coming at us from multiple agencies, but I don't want them to have access to our software."

"It was simple really," Bit said after wiping his fingers. With each bite of his burger, he used his napkin. He was following her lead, and should something take place this evening, he would have her back. "I've created separate portals for each agency, and all they have to do is upload their files. The software then compresses each—"

"How is Zoey?"

"Zoey?"

"Zoey," Brook reiterated before sticking the tongs of her fork into a steak fry. She then shot him a curious sideways glance.

"Your girlfriend? The one whose parents you are meeting when we get back home?"

"She's good." Bit cleared his throat. "I met her mother. Sort of. It was an accident really. Zoey and I were on a video call when there was a knock on her door. Her mother showed up unexpectedly. I was going to disconnect, but Mrs. Collins must have a sixth sense or something."

"All mothers have that sixth sense, Bit." Brook shook her head in what he assumed was amusement as she chose another fry. "Especially when it comes to their daughters."

"Yeah, well, Mrs. Collins made a beeline straight for Zoey's computer. She started peppering me with questions, and then she kept going on and on about how much she liked my taste in furniture. She then asked where I bought the beautiful antique table behind me."

Brook's fork hovered midair as she waited for his reply. When he couldn't bring himself to finish his story, he took a huge bite of his burger.

"You didn't, Bit." Brook lowered the utensil until it rested on the paper of the plastic basket that held her food. "Tell me you did not lie to Zoey's mother."

"I panicked," Bit exclaimed around a mouthful of food. He chewed for a moment, not expecting Brook to laugh. When he first met her, she never even cracked a smile. "I told her that I found it at a yard sale, which she took to mean that I love those kinds of things. One thing led to another, and the next thing I know—are you still laughing? This isn't funny, Boss. What am I going to do? I can't spend an entire weekend walking around looking at junk."

By this time, Brook had set her fork down completely in exchange for her napkin, which she was using to dab the corners of her eyes. He had been serious about his question.

"Can I get you a refill?"

Seeing as Brook wasn't going to answer the waitress, Bit nodded his reply followed by asking for more ketchup. He would have swiped a bottle from another table, but the place was packed. There wasn't one table available.

"I would advise you to tell Zoey's mother the truth, but I don't think you'll take that recommendation." Brook still had a grin on her face as she reached for her fork. "Bit, you never cease to amaze me."

He waited for her to continue, because it was obvious from her expression that she was going to say more on the subject. Yet there was a subtle shift in her body language that had him turning his focus toward Mary Jane.

Only it hadn't been Mary Jane who had captured Brook's attention.

"How were the chicken tenders and double order of loaded fries you had for lunch?"

"Fantastic," Bit replied to the waitress who worked at the Crestlake Bar & Grill. He remembered her name was Mindy and that she had been the one to hand him his lunch. "I noticed that you threw in some extra barbeque sauce. I appreciate that."

"No problem." Mindy flashed a smile toward Brook, who simply nodded her greeting in response. Mindy peered over her shoulder toward Mary Jane. "Has there been any progress on the case?"

"Yes."

Mindy quickly turned back to meet Brook's gaze.

"Really?"

Brook remained silent, and Bit shifted awkwardly in his seat when the two women continued to stare at one another. Mindy began to alter her position with discomfort, as well.

"I'm glad to hear it," Mindy said after a moment of strained silence. "I hope you catch the guy. I, um, I was just going to the restroom."

Brook monitored Mindy's progression to the small hallway near the back, not removing any scrutiny until the restroom door closed behind the woman. Bit waited for any instructions in silence.

"Who is Mindy here with tonight?" Brook asked Bit before their waitress returned with their drinks. It wasn't until after she had returned to the bar that Brook continued her line of questioning and the reason behind it. "Do you recognize anyone from the Crestlake Bar & Grill? Mindy walked through the front door and directly toward the restroom as she scanned the faces of those inside."

The fact that Brook would even ask him those questions meant that she hadn't recognized anyone present whom they had already met at the pier. He was confident that Brook had already memorized every face in the joint.

"I don't see anyone," Bit replied after he glanced around the establishment. He then pushed away what remained of his food. He had pretty much polished off his burger, anyway. "I'll know for sure when I get back to the van."

"Where did you park?"

"Directly across from the front entrance of the bar," Bit said before flashing Brook a smile. "Once you told me why the plans had changed, I made sure to load everything up in the van while we were here. We'll have hours of footage to go through when we get back to the lake house. I'll also run the footage through our facial recognition program. Anyone who came here tonight will be run against those people at the pier."

"I think most everyone will match given the crowd," Brook replied wryly as she tossed her napkin into the small plastic basket. "Still, I have to commend you, Bit. That was excellent planning and a reminder that you should be out in the field more often."

Bit wasn't so sure about her last statement, because he was a lot more comfortable behind his computer screens. Granted, he had been in the field here and there, but it wasn't his preferred place to be during an active investigation.

"When Mindy comes out of the restroom, we can see who she joins afterward," Bit pointed out as he took the straw from his glass of ice and slid it into his new soda. He finally understood the direction of Brook's thoughts. "You don't think Mindy is working with the unsub, but you think the unsub might be using others to his advantage without their knowledge."

"Such a tactic would fit his profile," Brook murmured before they both fell quiet, waiting for Mindy to reappear from the restroom.

A part of Bit wished Mindy hadn't interrupted his conversation with Brook. It was rare that they spent time together without the others around, and he always valued her input when it came to any type of advice. While she was right that he should try and rectify the misunderstanding that he had gotten himself into with Zoey's mother, doing so might damage the rapport the two of them had already established over the video call.

"Mary Jane and Adam are getting ready to leave."

Brook leaned back against the high-top chair as she discreetly observed the couple. Bit noticed two things at once—Adam Bouras stood to pull out Mary Jane's chair while the federal agent at the bar casually reached into his back pocket and pulled out his wallet. The man's movements weren't hurried, and no one detected that his imminent departure was based on Mary Jane Reynold's decision to leave the bar.

It wasn't long before the couple stood at the door with Adam getting ready to open an umbrella. The rain was still coming down in torrents, though there appeared to be less lightning than when Bit had first arrived. As the door was about to close behind them, the federal agent somehow managed to join them without anyone the wiser.

Bit turned to monitor the door to the restroom when the air shifted at the table. He wasn't sure how or why, especially considering that Brook hadn't altered her expression in any way, but something had caught her attention.

"Boss?"

Brook slowly set her club soda down on the table. The restroom door opened to reveal Mindy, and her face lit up with recognition. Her smile grew as she continued to walk across the hardwood floor of the bar. Bit followed her progression until she reached...Cav Buckley.

The man must have entered the establishment right after Mary Jane's exit. No wonder Bit had sensed a change in Brook. It didn't help that Cav peered over Mindy's shoulder and purposely winked in Brook's direction.

"Boss, I don't know why Cav Buckley is back in town, but he had alibis for the first three murders." Bit understood the need for further verification, but he was one hundred percent confident that the lawyer had nothing to do with their case. "I have security footage from one work event, plus two nightclubs for the other evenings in question. The man likes to drink, party, and flaunt his money."

"I don't think that Cav Buckley is here because of Mary Jane Reynolds," Brook replied softly as she reached for her purse. Bit wasn't sure exactly what she meant by that statement, but there was an edge to her tone. Normally, she would have paid the bill with a credit card to expense the meal when they got back to the city. Instead, she pulled out a fifty-dollar bill before securing the money with her glass of club soda. "I need to take care of something, Bit. I'll meet you back at the lake house."

Brook made no move to leave the table, and it was obvious that she was waiting for him to leave. He stood, grabbed his phone, and then removed the keys from the front pocket of his jeans. He thought over the information that had been in Cav Buckley's background check, but the only thing of interest had been a restraining order filed by a woman over five years ago.

Bit assumed that it had been in relation to a domestic situation, but maybe there had been more to it than that.

Brook's slight nod of encouragement when he glanced her way had him finally turning away from the table. It was as if she was planning on doing something that she didn't want him either witnessing or taking part in. He could only assume that she wanted him to have some type of deniability, but whatever it was seemed to be going over his head.

"Bit?" Brook called out, stopping him maybe ten feet from their table. He turned around to find that she had stood from her chair and was in the middle of securing the strap of her purse over her shoulder. "I'll be home in thirty minutes."

"Copy, Boss."

Bit understood the meaning behind her statement. If she wasn't at the lake house in a half hour, he was to alert Agent Tirelli and local enforcement. He still wasn't sure exactly what she was planning on doing or what it had to do with Cav Buckley, but he would do as she requested because he trusted her...just as she trusted him.

CHAPTER NINETEEN

Brooklyn Sloane

May 2024

Saturday — 9:37 pm

THE BASS COMING FROM the speakers above the bar reverberated through the wooden floorboards as Brook weaved through the crowd. The rain had driven everyone indoors, and this was the next best place to be. Unfortunately, the air had become thick with the stench of sweat and alcohol. She was looking forward to breathing fresh air, but there was something she needed to take care of before driving back to the lake house.

"Excuse me," Brook murmured as she brushed past a couple deep in conversation about a popular movie.

She was determined to reach the empty stool left by the federal agent who had followed Mary Jane home. Since the stool was positioned at the far end of the bar near the wall, it would provide her with the privacy needed to get her point across.

Brook didn't bother to relinquish her purse. She kept the thick strap over her shoulder as she perched on the edge of the stool. She wouldn't be sitting for long, either.

The bartender moved toward her, but Brook raised a hand, palm out. She didn't plan on staying, and she wouldn't be enjoying a drink, either. What she wouldn't give for a hot cup of coffee, though.

Across the bar, Mindy was laughing at something Cav Buckley whispered into her ear. As expected, he was staring directly at Brook, his gaze lingering on her with an unsettling intensity. He wasn't obtuse, and he understood that she was waiting to have a private word with him. She didn't doubt that he would make her wait. Such a strategy would backfire, not that such a thought crossed his mind.

Five minutes turned into ten before Cav reached out and tucked a strand of Mindy's blonde hair behind her ear. He slowly began to make his way through the throng of people standing near the bar. There was no mistaking the confidence in his approach. Before too long, he was standing right next to her as he planted his forearms firmly against the counter.

"Imagine bumping into you here," Cav murmured as he leaned into Brook's space. A smile stretched across his face as if they were old friends reunited by chance. "I thought for sure you would have gone back to D.C."

"I'd like you to ask yourself a question, Mr. Buckley," Brook instructed in a flat tone. She had already made sure to stand, ensuring that her high heels gave her as much leverage as possible. "Do you value your freedom?"

Brook held his gaze. Twenty seconds was longer than one realized, but she didn't back down. As a matter of fact, she stepped close enough to ensure there were mere inches between them.

Cav Buckly craved control, similar to that of her brother. Cav wasn't a killer, though. He was nowhere near the level of Jacob Walsh, but the underlying tendencies of obsession were just beneath the surface. Brook refused to be hunted by a stalker with sociopathic tendencies. She would do what was necessary to end the man's fixation.

"I have no idea what you're talking about," Cav replied softly, his warm breath containing the scent of spearmint. Too bad, really. She wasn't sure she would ever be able to enjoy that specific mint in the future. "And may I remind you that I'm a lawyer?"

"And may I remind you that I'm the sister of a serial killer?" Brook slowly smiled, though she made sure it conveyed her message. She allowed the silent challenge to hang between them for a moment. "I know all about the complaints at your firm. Most were brushed under the rug, but Talia Katics? She wouldn't back down, and that restraining order she was awarded also got her a settlement, didn't it? You have a history, Mr. Buckley. One that displays a pattern that I won't be a part of, do you understand me?"

Brook allowed a moment of measured silence to hover between them. He was staring at her lips, as if he were mesmerized by the subtle coat of her lipstick. She noticed the moment her words registered in his mind due to his gaze lifting to meet hers.

"Those were nothing more than misunderstandings."

"You and I both know better, so consider this a courtesy warning. I assure you, a restraining order will seem like a love letter compared to the measures that I'll take if I see you again," Brook warned as she finally allocated space between them. His smile had faltered the moment she had brought up her knowledge of his past. "I trust this is the last time that we'll meet, Mr. Buckley."

Brook's words hung in the air, and she noticed the twitch of irritation in the muscle alongside his jawline. Without another word, Brook brushed past him, her movements fluid and precise without the slightest hesitation. She didn't bother to glance over her shoulder at Cav as she made her way past the multitude of patrons who were lost in their own worlds. She had done what she set out to do, and she had categorically gotten her point across.

Stepping out into the cool night, Brook allowed herself a single deep breath, not caring that she was now getting soaked with rain. Men like Buckley became focused on an individual, and nothing but extreme action could shake their attention. Stalkers had a lot of traits similar to serial killers. Unfortunately, there were times when nothing said or done could prevent the situation from escalating into a grave situation. Only time would tell if Cav Buckley made the right decision.

The comparison between stalkers and serial killers brought her up short. Brook had made such similarities in her current profile, but she hadn't focused on that specific fact. While Mary Four was the unsub's current obsession, Sheila Wallace was where it all started. Again, the team was more than aware of that fact, but Bit needed to dive deeper into the woman's life.

The answers were there...just waiting to be found.

Nothing seemed out of place as she began to walk toward her car, the rain soaking her suit jacket. She didn't detect anyone in the vicinity. By the time she settled in behind the steering wheel, her brief moment of freedom from the stifling confrontation inside the bar had been replaced with a chill that not even the heated seats in her car could erase. Once she had the engine started with her phone connected to Bluetooth, she immediately initiated a call to Bit.

"Bit, I'm leaving the bar now," Brook advised as she shifted the gear into drive. "Mind brewing up a pot of coffee for me? It's going to be a long night."

CHAPTER TWENTY

Sylvie Deering

May 2024

Monday — 8:37 am

A FAINT FETID MILDEW made itself known as Sylvie pushed through the glass door of an aging office building located in the heart of downtown Ann Arbor. There were hints of upgrades here and there, but its history remained intact for the most part.

Fred Dawkins had postponed their initial meeting, not that he had bothered to call Sylvie before she had arrived at his place of work. He had phoned later Saturday night to apologize and reschedule their meeting for Monday morning at nine o'clock. She had intentionally arrived early, not wanting a repeat of Saturday.

"Bit, have you confirmed that Cav Buckley left town?" Sylvie asked, adjusting her cell phone so that the strand of hair that escaped her bun didn't get caught against her ear. "The man's history when it comes to fixating on someone speaks volumes. Brook needs to take this seriously."

"From what Boss told me Saturday night, she took care of it. I also called Buckley's office this morning, asking to speak with him. The receptionist patched me through, but I disconnected when he answered the call." There was a pause before Bit confirmed Sylvie's suspicion. "I was able to verify his departure another way too, but I know you're about to meet up with Dawkins. There's no need to go into specific details."

"That's probably for the best," Sylvie murmured as she glanced to her right. She had spotted a small coffee shop on Saturday, but the place had been closed for the weekend. Given the number of patrons sitting at the tables and those lingering near the condiment area, it was the go-to place during the work-week. "Thanks for the update, Bit. I'll let you know if Dawkins adds anything of importance to the investigation."

Bit made it sound as if Brook had put the confrontation with Buckley behind her. Sylvie couldn't shake her unease. The encounter had revealed just how far the man was willing to go for Brook's attention. Would her warning only serve to pique Buckley's interest, or had her veiled threat successfully deterred him? Sylvie trusted that Brook would let everyone know if she suspected the latter.

Sylvie made her way over to the short line in front of the cafe's cash register. The lull promised a swift transaction, and she seized the opportunity. When it was her turn to place her order, which was her usual Chai tea, she also added a hot coffee. She would attempt to use it as liquid encouragement in hopes of acquiring Fred Dawkins' trust.

The barista had both beverages ready in under a minute. Sylvie politely asked for a holder before securing both cups. She then retraced her steps toward the elevator bank. While she waited for the doors to slide open, she thought over the interviews that she and Theo had been able to conduct yesterday at the hospital. The administrative staff had nothing useful to add, leaving Theo and Sylvie back at the hotel for most of the afternoon performing some administrative duties of their own.

Theo was currently attempting to locate Shane Dawkins. The social worker's son had all but dropped off the map after college. Not even Bit had been able to locate him through social media, financials, or other online footprints.

As Sylvie stepped out onto the appropriate floor, she hadn't expected to find a sea of cubicles spanning the entire level. Phones were constantly ringing, no one was afforded private conversations, and voices were being raised to ensure no one misunderstood what was being said. Not one private office had been constructed with a scenic view. As for her sense of smell, it was accosted by the stench of burnt coffee.

"Excuse me," Sylvie said, ensuring her voice was heard over the nearest conversation. "I'm looking for Fred Dawkins."

A middle-aged woman didn't bother to stop her progress across the floor. She pointed toward the back of the room without saying a word, either.

"Dawkins is the first cubicle on the left-hand side at the far end," a male subject said as he spun his chair around to face her. He flashed a smile as he held the receiver of his desk phone to his ear. "Unless I can help you."

"Thanks, anyway," Sylvie said, returning his smile. He was only being friendly, very unlike the disposition of Cav Buckley. "Have a good day."

She began to advance down the thin aisle separating the cubicles. No one gave her a second glance. Once she reached the designated cubicle, she recognized the man occupying the space immediately. He was in his mid-fifties, though there wasn't a streak of gray in his jet-black hair.

"...an exception? The kid just turned six years old last month. His mother overdosed and is in the hospital for the next few days. We're talking about a week max," Fred pleaded as he rubbed his temple having no idea that Sylvie was standing at the entrance of his cubicle. "No, the boy's father is in prison. No grandparents, aunts, or uncles are on record."

Fred's shoulders relaxed somewhat upon hearing the response that he so clearly wanted...needed...to have in order for a six-year-old boy to have a safe place to stay for the time being.

"Thank you, Mrs. Nestine. I'll pick Kyle up from the hospital and bring him to you in a few hours. See you soon."

Fred lowered the receiver, finally catching sight of Sylvie's shadow. He didn't startle, but it was evident by the surprise on his face that he had been expecting a coworker. His glance at the computer screen to note the time gave credence to her assumption.

"You must be Sylvie Deering," Fred said as he quickly stood from his chair. He shook her hand before gesturing toward the black chair that had been positioned tight against his filing cabinet. "Please, have a seat."

"I know that I'm a few minutes early," Sylvie said as she removed a cup of coffee from the cardboard holder, extending it toward him. "After Saturday's appointment was rescheduled, I didn't want to take any chances. I'm in from out of town."

"I didn't even think to ask," Fred said ruefully as he took the proffered cup. He waited until she was sitting comfortably before he reclaimed his own chair. "I apologize for making you stay the weekend. I was on call this weekend, and—"

"No need to apologize, Mr. Dawkins." Sylvie placed her purse underneath her chair before handing over the cupholder to Fred. He tossed it in the small trashcan underneath his desk, not noticing that she had removed a piece of paper that she had tucked inside her purse. "I was just implying that meeting with you earlier will be beneficial to both of us."

"On the phone, you mentioned that you wanted to discuss Sheila Wallace." Fred opened his desk drawer and pulled out two pink sugar packets. "Why is the FBI investigating Sheila?

She not only died a year ago, but she removed herself from fostering children at least a decade ago, if not longer."

"Was there anyone who would have wanted to hurt Sheila?"

"Hurt?" Fred had removed the white lid from his coffee cup, but his motions stilled when he assumed that Sylvie meant Sheila had been murdered. Sylvie didn't bother to correct him. She had been through this same conversation multiple times. "I had heard that Sheila died from a stroke."

"I realize that the last time you spoke with Ms. Wallace was over a decade ago, but can you recall anyone who would have wanted to harm her? A foster child? A biological parent?"

Sylvie and Theo had gone down a rabbit hole last night, because the motive was subjective at this point in the investigation. Had Sheila Wallace abused one of her foster children? Did a biological parent want revenge on the system? Was someone from the original recipient's family livid over their loved one dying because someone else was given Wallace's heart?

The team needed to find a way to narrow down their suspect list.

"Mr. Dawkins, I spoke with Andrea Simpson, Tyler Doss, and Mitch Swilling on Saturday. They shared their experiences in that home. Sheila Wallace wasn't the best foster parent, and it's my understanding that you were well aware of that fact."

Fred Dawkins had finished pouring the two sugar packets into his coffee, but he made no move to pick up his beverage. Since he was clean-shaven, it was hard not to notice the way he was gritting his teeth. He finally met her gaze with disgust.

"This job...these kids...we do the best we can. Sheila wasn't the best foster parent, but she sure as hell wasn't the worst. For some, her home was better than the alternative."

"I couldn't do what you do on a daily basis, Mr. Dawkins," Sylvie said softly, knowing that their conversation was probably being listened to by others. It would have been ideal to have this conversation in private, but this floor didn't even have a conference room. "Just as I'm sure you would say the same thing about my job. I'm not here to judge you for the decisions you made then or now. I just need a list of foster children who would be twenty-five to thirty-five years of age today who had been in Ms. Wallace's care."

Sylvie set her Chai tea down on the small filing cabinet and unfolded the warrant. She then handed it to him without hesitation.

"We were able to secure a warrant for any information on those who fall inside the requirements." Sylvie gave Dawkins a moment to review the document. It provided her time to reach back into her purse and pull out one of her business cards. Once she had placed it on the corner of his desk, she picked up her Chai tea in hopes of keeping the meeting civil. "I'll ask you again, Mr. Dawkins. Is there any foster child who harbored enough animosity towards Sheila Wallace that they might have been driven to extreme action?"

"No." Fred cleared his throat as he leaned back in his chair. "Some had tempers, some were resentful, but I don't believe any of them would have physically harmed Sheila."

Sylvie didn't bother to correct his assumption that this was regarding Sheila Wallace's death. Sylvie needed to steer the topic of conversation toward Dawkins' son, but she wanted to do so in a manner that wouldn't shut down the discussion.

"When I visited with Andrea, Tyler, and Mitch, they mentioned that you used to bring your son to the youth center once a week." Sylvie kept her tone conversational. "Shane became close with the children you helped over the years, is that a correct assumption?"

"I raised my son to help others less fortunate." The lines around Fred's eyes softened when he spoke of Shane. "Yes, I used to bring him to the youth center. Kids respond to other kids. They trust one another in ways that they don't adults, which is understandable. These children end up in the system because the adults who they were supposed to count on failed in their responsibilities."

"We've attempted to locate Shane, but we can't seem to find an address for him. We're hoping that he remembers someone or maybe even recalls a conversation that might help us in our investigation."

"Ms. Deering, I haven't seen my son in years." Fred visibly swallowed as he wrapped his hand around the disposable cup. Once he was in control of his emotions, he continued speaking. "Shane dropped out of college, started living on the streets, and he cut all ties with me and his mother. We tried getting him help, but..."

Sylvie couldn't imagine dedicating her life to helping children, only to lose her own child. She wasn't sure what had prompted Shane to leave behind college, his friends, or his family. Observing Fred's body language, she wasn't sure that even he understood where it had all gone wrong.

"I wish I could help you, but as I already stated, I did my best to place children where I thought they stood the best chance of making it to their eighteenth birthday. The truth? I didn't like Sheila Wallace. No one working in this office was fond of the woman, but she never physically abused the kids placed in her home."

Sylvie's stomach churned at the way Fred attempted to assuage his choices. His small speech spoke to his knowledge of neglect. It was clear from his words that he had placed older children in Wallace's care who he thought could handle such mental and emotional abuse.

Fred glanced down at his desk. She caught his slight hesitation when he reached for her business card. He was withholding information from her. This moment was the first time since she sat down that she had hope for a break in the case.

"It will take me a couple of days to gather the requested files," Fred said reluctantly as he tucked her card into his keyboard so that it was facing him. There was something in his mannerisms that suggested he was about to divulge an important detail. It didn't help that the fluorescent lights caused his features to appear rigid. "As you read through the records, you need to remember that teenagers embellish facts...make accusations. I would like to reiterate that I did my due diligence on Sheila Wallace's home and discovered nothing that would suggest she physically abused those children placed in her home."

Sylvie barely managed to contain the spark of anger that originated upon hearing his statement. He was suggesting that one or more of the teens placed in Wallace's home suggested otherwise. Had they mentioned something damning in their interviews, only to then be ignored?

"Mr. Dawkins, whose file will I discover such accusations?"

"Mitch Swilling."

Sylvie thought back to Mitch's reaction to her line of questioning. He had been the one to suggest that Wallace's home hadn't been ideal, but he had implied it had been better than most. When she had purposefully brought up Fred Dawkins, Mitch's bitterness had been undeniable. Something had transpired between them, and the details were in those files.

CHAPTER TWENTY-ONE

Brooklyn Sloane

May 2024

Monday — 10:37 am

"I UPLOADED THE FOOTAGE from the van," Bit said as he reached for another donut out of the opened box. "I've been over it twice, and I've separated the individuals who are regulars at the Crestlake Bar & Grill. Nothing stands out, though."

Brook narrowed her gaze on the box until she was confident Bit hadn't taken the last chocolate donut. She should have known that he would take the raspberry jelly one since those were his favorite.

"I've been thinking about that, and I might go back to Mary Jane's neighborhood to canvas the neighborhood once more. Our unsub is still looking for an opportunity to reach her without being caught. If the unsub is under the impression that Janice Morris' death was simply collateral damage, there is a good chance that he'll try the same method again...especially if he believes law enforcement won't double back and ensure the safety of the community."

Patrol cars were not going to be enough to deter someone like their killer. His patience was unlimited, and he wouldn't be prevented from monitoring his target, regardless that law enforcement was breathing down his neck. He would do everything in his power to outsmart those hunting him.

"I thought the local police were doing welfare checks every day." Bit had already eaten half his donut. He used the back of his hand to wipe away the powdered sugar that remained on his upper lip. "Speaking of welfare checks, Big T checked in when you were in the kitchen. He stopped in at every shelter in Ann Arbor. Shane Dawkins hasn't been seen in years. Oh, and the warrant Big T submitted for additional hospital security footage came through, but only for the elevator banks that have access to the ICU. Big T is at the hospital now."

Brook turned back to face the portable monitor, her hands wrapped around a porcelain mug. The warmth from her freshly brewed coffee seeped into her palms.

"I've read the update from the local police department, but I'd feel more comfortable checking on those neighbors myself."

Brook took a moment to study their handiwork on the screen. She and Bit had spent the morning segregating the software program to include three branches of the investigation—Sheila Wallace, Reggie Hollins, and those involved with the transplant team.

"What about Sylvie?" Brook asked as she stepped forward and pressed on a specific file. Mitch Swilling's picture appeared, taken from the last time he renewed his driver's license. "I know that she was attempting to locate Swilling, but did she go with Theo to the hospital?"

"Little T is currently pulling up to Andrea Simpson's residence." Bit had everyone's location at his fingertips based on their phone's GPS. "Sylvie mentioned that Andrea has been in touch with Mitch, so she should know where he has been staying while in town. I was of no help to Little T, because the man doesn't have an online presence."

The melody that usually alerted them to an incoming call came from one of the laptops. Brook wasn't surprised to find the blue eyes of a kitten suddenly staring back at her. The white kitten reached out to tap Arden's phone with her paw, causing Bit to converse with the furball in a high-pitched tone.

"Look at you. Look at those blue eyes. You are so—"

"Sylvie's here, Arden."

The phone bobbled and eventually fell with a thud. Brook turned to find Bit standing on the other side of the table with his mouth open. She shrugged, fighting a smile as she lifted the rim of her coffee cup to her lips.

"Gumshoe, that's not true! Little T is in Ann Arbor."

Brook's phone chimed from the coffee table.

"I'm turning sixty-eight this year, Brook," Arden reminded her in a stern voice, though there was humor shimmering in his dark eyes. He must have been holding the kitten for a while, because there was white fur attached to his brown cardigan sweater. "I'd like to stick around for a while."

"Arden, I have a feeling you'll be around long after me." Brook retrieved her phone. Reading the name on the display, she began to walk toward the kitchen. "You two go crazy over the office mascot while I take this call. Oh, and Arden? You might want to invest in a lint roller."

Brook swiped the screen of her phone to accept the call.

"Sloane," Brook announced as she entered the kitchen.

"It's Dever. Do you have a minute?"

Brook could hear the gravity in the federal agent's voice. The brusque tone had her setting her coffee mug on the counter. If he was going to tell her that the search for Stella Bennett's remains turned up nothing, Brook was going to need some fresh air.

"Yes."

Though the forecast had promised an overcast sky, the sun was currently bathing the wooden planks in warmth. Not even the heat from the golden rays could chase away the cold that settled in her bones. Seeing as it would be near impossible to sit while listening to the results of the search, she crossed the deck to stand at the railing.

"We found the remains of a young girl."

Brook wrapped her left hand around the weathered wood, needing something to hold onto that would anchor her for the rest of the conversation. She usually spun the outer band of her worry ring when needing some semblance of comfort, but she was afraid that she would drop her phone.

"Stella Bennett?"

"We won't know for sure until we are able to transport the remains to the lab, but I'm being told the bones belong to a young female between the ages of ten and twelve." Dever paused, allowing Brook the needed time to gather her thoughts. She wasn't the type of woman who wished upon a shooting star or had faith in something she couldn't see with her own eyes...but this moment made her want to be that woman. "Even though the camp has been closed for over a decade, most of the buildings are still standing. We discovered the remains under the wooden planks of the cabin you advised where your brother stayed with a group of other boys."

"Far left corner?" Brook managed to ask while her pulse throbbed in her temples. "Underneath a bed?"

"From the marks on the floor, yes. The furniture was moved out of this place long ago." Dever must have pulled the phone away from his face, because his words became muffled and weren't directed at her. She was grateful for the reprieve to remind herself to breathe. "First impressions are that the body was wrapped in plastic. Sealed tight. It would explain why no odor was detected in the weeks following her death."

Brook's brother had only been eleven years old when Stella Bennett had officially been reported missing by her uncle. In the long hours that the campers were attempting to locate a lost boy from camp, Jacob had found the time to brutally commit his first murder. Given his high IQ, it wasn't shocking that he would know how to hide a body while disguising the odor at such a young age.

Something in Jacob's mind hadn't snapped that day. Plastic? Enough to seal the body of a young girl? The materials and hiding spot proved premeditation.

"I'll hold off notifying Special Agent Houser until we are given a positive ID. Still, given everything that we know right now? I think it's safe to say Jacob Walsh will stand trial and receive the death penalty."

"Thank you, Rick."

Such formalities of gratitude were inadequate, but that was all she had at the moment. She disconnected the call, but she didn't move from the railing. Remaining in place, she slowly raised her face to bask in the warmth of the sun.

Had this moment arrived three years ago, Brook wasn't sure what her reaction would have been to the news. She had been so isolated back then. Her entire existence had revolved around her brother.

In a way, Jacob was the one responsible for the changes in her life. His obsessive need to check in on her from time to time had prompted her to break the consulting agreement she had with the Bureau. And when Graham had made her an offer that she couldn't refuse...it had been like taking her first breath after being suffocated for so long.

Brook brought her head forward so that she could access her phone.

The line trilled, but only once.

His deep voice caressed her ear and brought a smile to her face.

"They found her, Graham. They discovered Stella Bennett's remains."

CHAPTER TWENTY-TWO

Sylvie Deering

May 2024

Monday — 10:49 am

CLOUDS FLOATED LAZILY ACROSS the sky, allowing rays of sunlight to drift intermittently across the SUV's dashboard. The thunderstorms had moved out of the area late last night. Given that the storm front had taken with it the humidity, there was a slight chill that lingered in the morning air.

Sylvie had dropped Theo off at the hospital around twenty minutes ago. Theo had wanted to obtain security footage of the hospital's elevator banks that served the ICU. While the recordings would be forwarded to Bit for further analysis, Theo preferred to examine the three-day footage himself to quickly ascertain if any of the suspects they had on their list had attempted to visit Sheila Wallace.

"Damn it," Sylvie muttered as she stared down at the tablet in her hands.

She had read through the case files that Fred Dawkins had emailed her the other day. As a matter of fact, she had gone over them multiple times, but she was just now noticing that a page had been left out of Mitch Swilling's file. Just to make sure that she wasn't missing a specific section of Mitch's history somewhere, she closed out the document and gently pressed the screen to regain access.

There was no denying that the file wasn't complete.

Sylvie glanced out the passenger side window. She was currently parked outside of Andrea Simpson's residence. Sylvie's intention was to locate Mitch Swilling. The only one who had that information was Andrea, but Sylvie would prefer to be armed with as much information as possible.

With a sigh of resignation, Sylvie reached into her purse. She had already turned the engine off, so her phone was no longer connected to the Bluetooth. She exited the document once more to access Fred Dawkins' contact information. Once it was on the screen, she pressed the corresponding numbers.

Holding the phone to her ear, she listened to the dull, repetitive ring. After several peals, she was met with Dawkins' voicemail. Sylvie kept the irritation from her voice as she explained the situation. She disconnected the line after requesting that he email her the missing documents as soon as possible.

With no immediate way to fill in the blanks, Sylvie tucked her tablet into her purse. She pulled the key from the ignition, secured the strap of her purse over her shoulder, and stepped out of the SUV. Just in case Fred called back, she kept ahold of her phone as she shut the driver's side door.

The suburban neighborhood was quiet this time of the morning. Not even the distant hum of a lawnmower could be heard in the distance. Sylvie walked up the driveway, toward the thin pathway that led to the front door. She raised her hand and knocked firmly.

After a few seconds, Sylvie could hear the shuffle of footsteps. The inner door opened, revealing Andrea Simpson. They might have been separated by the flimsy barrier of a screen door, but it was impossible to miss the way the woman tensed and became wary at the sight of her visitor.

"Ms. Deering. What are you doing back here?"

"I need to speak with you about Mitch Swilling." Sylvie opened the screen door, not wanting to give Andrea the chance to slam the door shut. "I have some follow-up questions for him, but we can't seem to locate him. Do you happen to know where he is staying?"

Andrea regarded Sylvie for a long moment before she released her hold on the doorknob. She opened the inner door wider, motioning for Sylvie to enter the house.

"Why do you want to speak with Mitch?" The wariness in Andrea's tone suggested that she had invited Sylvie inside to collect more information. It wasn't all that hard to detect the edge in her tone...a protective one at that. "I'm sure I can answer anything that you need to know from back then."

Sylvie stepped over the threshold. The faint odor of cigarette smoke still lingered in the air, but the smell took a backseat to the burnt scent of toast. She didn't see any sign of food in the living room, though.

"You love him." Sylvie normally wouldn't have made such an assumption, but Andrea wasn't going to give up Mitch's location without good reason. Even then, there was a good chance that Sylvie left here without an address. "Don't you?"

Andrea crossed her arms as she stood near the couch. She didn't reply, but she also didn't meet Sylvie's knowing stare. There was only one avenue left for Sylvie, so she took it.

"Have you been watching the news lately? Keeping up on current events?" Sylvie asked before taking a seat in the same chair as she had on her previous visit. She set her purse in the same spot, only she kept her phone in her hand. "Three women named Mary Jane Reynolds have been murdered over the course of seven months. All of them resided in the state of Michigan. You see, a woman by the name of Mary Jane Reynolds was the recipient of Sheila Wallace's heart. Unfortunately, the killer wasn't privy to which Mary Jane Reynolds was the actual recipient. He has taken it upon himself to kill every single woman with that name until he finds his target...all to ensure that her heart stops beating."

"And you think Mitch murdered those women?" Andrea's features lost all color. Her response indicated that she had heard about the three previous murders, but she hadn't connected them to Sheila. If Mitch was their unsub, he hadn't mentioned the name Mary Jane Reynolds to Andrea. "Mitch isn't a killer. I don't know why you would believe he is capable of murdering someone, but you're wrong."

"Andrea, someone doesn't want Sheila's heart to beat any longer," Sylvie stressed as she pushed a little harder. "I'm not accusing Mitch of being that person, but I do need to speak with him. Mitch made some previous claims about Sheila, but Fred Dawkins indicated that the stories were embellished at the time. All I want to do is verify the information that I received from social services."

"What claims? Because I don't believe that Mitch would have said anything that the rest of us didn't say back then," Andrea protested as she lowered her arms and finally sat on the couch. "Sheila had strict rules. As long as we adhered to them, she let us be. She didn't care what we did or where we went, as long as we followed her house rules. As we told you the other day, there were worse places to be. We all grew up and went our own way. None of us are capable of murder, though."

The room seemed to contract around them. They were at a crossroads. It didn't appear that Andrea was going to give up Mitch's location, but Sylvie wasn't ready to walk away just yet. She needed some time to think of another approach.

"Would you mind getting me some water?" Sylvie asked with a small smile, attempting to ease the tension in the room. "I'd also like to use your bathroom, if you don't mind."

"Sure," Andrea replied as she stood from the couch. She gestured toward the small hallway in front of the foyer. "Through there. I'll be in the kitchen."

"Thank you."

Sylvie advanced across the living room, noting that the small hallway most likely led to the kitchen from the other side. Andrea, on the other hand, had walked directly through the living and underneath the arch, disappearing from view. Sylvie didn't need the facilities, but she did use the time to wash her hands in the bathroom sink. Doing so gave her time to think of another way to obtain Mitch's current location.

As Sylvie exited the bathroom, she retraced her steps toward the living room. She hesitated when she spotted a small, thin latch underneath the staircase. Coming to a stop, she inspected what at first appeared to be a wall, the kind with white wooden panels that followed the sharp incline of the staircase. Only this wall had what appeared to be a small door. Since the latch had been painted white, the metal had blended into the background.

Sylvie hesitated, compelled to find out what was behind the wooden panels. She certainly didn't have a warrant to search the premises, but she had also been invited inside. In all likelihood, Andrea used the space as a storage area for additional rolls of toilet paper and extra hand towels.

"What are you doing?"

Sylvie glanced to her left, but she hadn't been startled by Andrea's appearance. The soles of her shoes could be heard crossing the kitchen tile. In her hand was a glass of ice water.

"I could lie and tell you that I was admiring the wooden paneling, but I won't." Sylvie had been given her answer as to what was behind the panels from Andrea's horrified reaction. "What's behind this door, Andrea? What will I find if I open—"

"Get out," Andrea yelled, not noticing that water had spilled over the rim of the glass. "Get out! Now!"

"I'll leave, Andrea." Sylvie kept her voice calm and even. "If that's what you would like, I'll collect my purse and leave. You should know that I will submit for a search warrant, though. You can either show me what is behind this door now or I'll be back in a few hours."

Everything the team had uncovered thus far led back to Sheila Wallace. This home had been her residence. Had Andrea Simpson not reacted in such a panicked manner, Sylvie might have returned to the living room to continue their conversation.

"You're going to assume the worst, and you won't believe me after..."

Andrea shook her head before disappearing around the corner. She was still visibly upset. Sylvie waited a moment longer, releasing the tension in her shoulders when Andrea came back into view sans the glass of water.

"I will listen to you, Andrea," Sylvie murmured in reassurance as Andrea came to a stop a few steps away. "Whatever you have to tell me, I promise to listen without reservation. In turn, I need you to trust me that I'm not accusing Mitch of any wrongdoing. I just need his help in clarifying some statements he made when he was younger."

"None of us are capable of murder."

Andrea was still in denial.

Sylvie couldn't say one way or another that the woman was wrong, but motive played a vital part in this investigation. Typically, serial killers had signatures, targeted specific victims, and couldn't bring themselves to stop. The unsub in this case was fueled by a goal. Once that goal was achieved, the unsub would blend back into the woodwork, never to be seen or heard from again.

Andrea finally nodded her consent. Sylvie slowly reached out to turn the small knob. It wasn't easy to get the latch to budge. As a matter of fact, Sylvie had to apply a lot of pressure for the bolt to release, suggesting that the space hadn't been used for quite some time.

Sylvie pulled the door open, and the height of it didn't even reach her chest. There didn't seem to be a light switch, so Sylvie lifted her phone and pressed the flashlight button on the display. The beam sliced through the darkness.

Nausea hit the back of her throat.

"It's not what it looks like," Andrea exclaimed, stepping forward until Sylvie shot her a warning glance. "It isn't. We told you the truth. Sheila didn't physically abuse us in any way. That alcove was just used as a time-out. A reminder that if we didn't follow her rules, we could be sent somewhere worse."

"Mental abuse is just as bad as physical abuse, Andrea."

The walls bore the scars of desperate expressions—drawings that told stories of sorrow and solitude. In the corner lay a tattered blanket, a stained pillow, and an old flashlight. Battery acid could be seen staining the side of the yellow plastic. The items were the remnants of a childhood prison.

"Answer me this, Andrea," Sylvie implored as she took pictures of the small space with her phone. She uploaded them to the firm's software, which would then send an alert to the team that images had been added to the case file. "Who spent the most time in there?"

Sylvie didn't need Andrea to respond, but forcing the woman to open her eyes to reality was paramount. The question hung between them until Andrea swiped at the tears that threatened to fall.

"Mitch, but you already knew that," Andrea responded bitterly. "He didn't murder anyone. He and Tyler were the only ones who never left me. I would know if one of them was capable of murder."

"Why haven't you cleaned that room out, Andrea?"

"Because it's easier to pretend it never existed," Andrea practically whispered as she stepped forward and slammed it shut.

"Mitch promised to help me fix up the place. It's one of the reasons that he is back in town, but he said he had to take care of something first. I'm assuming that it has to do with one of his brothers."

"Brothers?"

Sylvie suddenly realized what information had been missing from Mitch Swilling's file. While there was a section that explained Mitch's family history and how he came to be placed in foster care, the facts listed had been sparse. Mitch's mother had died of an overdose, and his father had been sent to prison for armed robbery.

"Ricky and Carl," Andrea replied as she brushed past Sylvie. "Ricky lives with his girlfriend in the apartment building near Wurster Park. Mitch usually stays with them when he's in town, which isn't often."

Sylvie was left to follow Andrea back into the living room. Since the federal field office was slammed with several cases and Agent Tirelli taking the lead on the Reggie Hollins' angle, she had yet to receive all the background checks on the foster children who would currently be in their late twenties or early thirties.

"And Carl?"

"I have no idea. Mitch hasn't mentioned him in years."

Andrea didn't take a seat. It was her way of letting Sylvie know that their conversation had finally come to an end. Sylvie collected her purse and walked toward the front entrance. She paused when her hand was on the handle.

"I got the sense that Tyler didn't know Mitch was in town. Why keep that information from Tyler if the three of you are so close?"

Andrea broke eye contact as she leaned down to pick up her cell phone from the coffee table. Sylvie was certain that Mitch would know to expect her within the next thirty minutes.

"I think I've already said enough," Andrea said as she began to close the distance between them. "You should leave now."

Sylvie gave a curt nod before pushing open the screen door and exiting the house. She had Theo on the line before ever reaching the driver's side door of the SUV.

"Can you wrap things up at the hospital?"

"Yes," Theo responded over low murmurs of conversations in the background. "I take it you found Mitch Swilling's location?"

"Even better," Sylvie stated as she settled in behind the steering wheel. She had already checked her surroundings upon walking down the short driveway, but she gave the area additional scrutiny before starting the engine. "We have two new suspects to add to our suspect list."

CHAPTER TWENTY-THREE

Brooklyn Sloane

May 2024

Monday — 1:03 pm

BROOK'S SHADOW STRETCHED LONG and thin across the wooden planks of the pier as she made her way towards the Crestlake Bar & Grill. The breeze was tinged with the scent of salt and fried food, and a partly cloudy sky loomed overhead, casting a subdued light on the early afternoon.

She wasn't just there to pick up lunch.

That was merely a pretext.

Her true motive was ensuring that Cav had taken her advice and left town. She had made the assumption—a correct one from his reaction the other night— that he had used Mindy to get closer to her. Brook couldn't in good conscience walk away without confirmation that Cav wouldn't transfer his sights to Mindy given her readiness to spend an evening with him.

Brook approached the bar, noting the lunch hour was still in full swing. Most of the tables were occupied, their laughter and conversation carrying through the air. It was easy to spot those who were taking a lunch break versus those who were enjoying a day off or on vacation. Clothes revealed a lot about a person. Those from the anchored boats alongside the pier were in swim trunks, swimsuits, or casual wear.

There were dirty plates and half-empty glasses on a few abandoned tables indicating the pace of the bar and grill during the past hour. Brook caught sight of a server near the far end of the pier. Unfortunately, the person wasn't who Brook wanted to speak with this afternoon.

Brook approached the bar, not bothering to walk toward the other end where the pick-up window was located for take-out orders. The bartender was methodically cataloging bottles and glasses behind the counter. He caught sight of her and flashed a smile.

"Is Mindy around?"

"Yeah, she's here," Chip replied as he set a clipboard on the counter. "She's covering for Jason again, so I can grab your takeout order."

"Thanks, I appreciate it," Brook said, her gaze drifting over to the side of the bar. The access to the kitchen was around the corner, but Mindy wasn't anywhere in sight. "If possible, I would appreciate it if you would let Mindy know that I'm here. I have something...personal...to discuss with her."

Brook stared at Chip, not intending to give him an explanation.

"Sure thing," Chip said as he began to stroll down to the other end of the bar. Brook followed his lead and came to stand in front of the pick-up counter as Chip stuck his head inside the kitchen. "Mindy! You have a visitor!"

Brook lifted her sunglasses until they pulled her hair back and were secured on top of her head. There was a warm breeze coming off the water, but she fortunately wasn't facing the glare of the sun. Mindy finally emerged from the kitchen, a gray bucket tucked against her hip.

"Mindy, I was hoping to speak with you in private for a moment," Brook said as she glanced toward Chip. He was gathering some plastic utensils and napkins to place into a white to-go bag that she assumed was her order. Bit had called in their lunch twenty minutes ago. "It's about the other night."

Mindy's gaze darted toward Chip in curiosity, but she nodded her agreement. She gestured toward the side of the structure. Brook made her way around the corner and waited patiently for Mindy to exit the kitchen. She had ditched the grey bucket.

"I have to ask," Mindy said hesitantly as she wrapped her arms around her abdomen. "Does Cav have something to do with your case? Is he..."

"No, no." Brook immediately dispelled Mindy's speculation. "Mr. Buckley has nothing to do with our investigation. I ran into him at an interview, and it came to my attention that a woman filed a restraining order against him five years ago."

Brook wasn't conveying any information that wasn't public knowledge. She was comfortable with warning Mindy about a man who had repetitive tendencies of harassing women. The reports to HR at his firm and the restraining order spoke volumes. Still, Brook was mindful of what details she divulged to Mindy.

"I realized that you were enjoying a Saturday evening with Mr. Buckley, but I couldn't in good conscience keep such information to myself." Brook paused to let her words sink in. "It's my hope that you stay clear of him, Mindy."

"Well, Cav left the bar right after you did that night," Mindy revealed as she relaxed her arms. She finally slipped her hands into the back pockets of her jeans. "I guess I should be thanking you. I met him when he was here with his friends. They were on some fishing vacation. When he called and said that he wanted to take me out for drinks, I certainly wasn't going to say no. Did you see his watch? That thing had to go for at least two grand."

Brook resisted the urge to rub her temple as a headache threatened to take hold. Cav had almost certainly been using Mindy as a way to be close to Brook, and Mindy had only accepted his invitation because she assumed that he was wealthy.

Cav Buckley lived paycheck to paycheck.

Those specific details were private, and Brook had already succeeded in warning Mindy of the man's proclivities. Should Mindy decide those predilections didn't matter, that was on her.

"I just thought you should know about the restraining order, Mindy. Do with that information what you will," Brook said with a nod before turning to collect her food. "Have a good day."

Brook rounded the corner to find her take-out bag ready and waiting. She reached into the pocket of her blazer and pulled out her cell phone. She opened the case before retrieving her credit card. Chip had been filling a chilled glass with draft beer, but she didn't have to wait long.

"Your colleague wanted extra bacon on his BLT, so that will be two dollars extra," Chip said as he took Brook's credit card.

"Do I want to know how many pieces he asked for?"

"He's asking for a heart attack," Chip replied with a laugh. He cashed out her order, but something he had said earlier had caught her attention. She waited until he handed her a pen and the small white receipt. "If it helps, I put in an extra side of fruit. Maybe that will counter—"

"Chip, you mentioned that Jason Bracco called in sick today?"

Brook quickly signed the receipt, not concerned about expensing the meal. Chip had stapled one to the bag.

"Yeah. And it's not like him to call off, either. I mean, Jason just got this job at the start of the season," Chip revealed as he turned around and tucked her signed receipt in the drawer of the cash register. "We'll be fine, though. I called Lucy in on her day off. She should be here any minute."

Brook didn't pick up the bag. She recalled Theo mentioning that Jason knew an awful lot about the locals, specifically Mary

Jane and Adam. If Jason was their unsub, why wouldn't he have targeted Mary Four first?

"Chip?" Brook had prevented him from returning to his duties behind the bar, so he held up a hand toward someone wanting a refill. "Mary Jane caused quite a stir with that video of hers. Was she posting those before her surgery?"

According to Bit, Mary Jane had her social media accounts before her surgery, but she only posted sporadically. It wasn't until after her heart transplant that she began to post regularly. It wouldn't hurt to have confirmation from a local.

"Surgery?" Chip frowned in confusion. "What surgery?"

"It's not important," Brook said, sidestepping his question. From her understanding, Jason was a local himself, or so they had all assumed. "Chip, I know this is an odd question, but how well do you know Jason?"

"Jason was raised in Crestlake. Went to college for some graphic design degree, got a job in Lansing, and then was laid off shortly thereafter."

"One more question," Brook said, noticing two men at the end of the bar becoming quite agitated with the wait. She reached into her pocket, flashing them her credentials to buy herself some more time. "Was Jason born in Crestlake?"

"Adopted, I think." Chip shifted his weight in a manner that suggested he was uneasy with her line of questioning. "Look, I'm sure Jason is just sick or something. Everyone knows his parents. He isn't going to make them look bad with the owner since they were the ones who got him this job in the first place."

There were several questions that Brook still needed to be answered, starting with Mary Jane. It was one thing to keep her surgery private when it came to social media, but to keep it from such a small community seemed to be a stretch.

Sylvie and Theo were currently tracking down Mitch Swilling. What if the theory that one of the man's biological brothers had some psychotic break was accurate? What if one of them blamed Sheila Wallace for not allowing all three brothers to be placed inside her home? Add to that discovery of how she treated Mitch, then said brother might do what was necessary to ensure that the woman's heart didn't continue to beat inside someone else.

"Thanks, Chip," Brook murmured as she quickly inserted her credit card back into its designated spot. She took a ten-dollar bill out from behind her phone and shoved it in the glass jar. She then tucked her phone case and credentials back into her pocket before swiping the to-go bag off the counter. "I hope your day gets better."

Brook began to retrace her steps, her heels not getting in the way of her quick pace. She wanted to get back to the lake house and submit background checks on all employees at the bar and grill, as well as the local bar.

Specifically, Jason Bracco.

Had one of Mitch Swilling's brothers been hiding in plain sight?

Chapter Twenty-Four

Brooklyn Sloane

May 2024

Monday — 1:37 pm

"...POSTED BY RICKY AUSTRY's girlfriend around the time that the two of them started dating. I can't find anything on Carl Swilling. He is almost as elusive as Shane Dawkins."

Brook quietly closed the door behind her as she followed Bit's gaze to the portable monitor. In the middle of the display was an old photograph containing three boys, ranging in age from eight to twelve years old. The picture had been taken on Halloween, if the costumes were anything to go by—a decaying zombie, a bloodthirsty vampire, and a fierce werewolf. Their makeup wasn't half bad, and it was obvious that someone had taken the time to help them with their outfits. Whoever had been behind the camera had captured a moment of mischief and excitement.

"The only one who is easy to make out is Mitch Swilling," Bit said as his gaze was drawn to the bag in Brook's hand. She set it on the table and began to unpack its contents. "He hasn't changed too much since then, but I figure this picture was taken a few years before his mother died from an overdose. I was able to reach someone else at social services, and since we had a warrant already in place, the woman forked over the files for Mitch Swilling's brothers. Once I explained the situation, I'm sure you'll be hearing from Dawkins sooner rather than later. By the way, he was in family court today, which was why you haven't been able to get in contact with him."

Bit tossed a pen back and forth in his hands as he began to wrap up the call. Brook took the time to crumple the white bag as she turned to study the picture that was to the left of Mitch Swilling's DMV photograph.

"Ricky is the youngest, which was probably why he took the Austry's surname. Carl was bounced around, fell in with some rough crowds, and never finished high school. I did manage to find his name connected with a call center for a wireless carrier. It's a small one, and they pay via a cash app," Bit said, pausing to hear Sylvie's side of the conversation. By this point, he had tossed his pen on the table and walked over to the food containers. "No address. Only a post office box located around thirty miles from here. I'm assuming Carl got one near his father's place so that he could pick up any mail. Mack Swilling made parole a couple of years ago."

Brook faced Bit, interested in hearing more about Carl Swilling. Her theory about Jason Bracco being the unsub was being pulled apart at the seams. She would still request that Bit look into him, as well as other employees at the bar and grill.

"Keep us posted, Little T." Bit pulled back his headset before readjusting his knit hat. He had already taken his meal back to his chair, but he didn't take his seat. "Those two are going to drive over to Ricky Austry's apartment. They're hoping to catch Mitch there. If he's not there, maybe Ricky can provide them with his brother's location. Oh, and Ricky Austry isn't our unsub. There are pictures on social media that provide him an alibi."

"What information came back on Mack Swilling?"

"The guy has been hopping from job to job. Constructions gigs, night shifts at warehouses, gas station clerk. You name it. There aren't many places willing to take a chance on an ex-con," Bit replied as he took the lid off his container. "Especially one convicted of armed robbery."

"You said that Mack Swilling lives thirty minutes from here?"

"Miles, so more like forty minutes with these roads." Bit ate a fry before wiping his fingers on a napkin. He then pressed a button on his keyboard, prompting her to focus on the monitor. "That is Mack Swilling's mug shot. Mitch is the spitting image of his father."

"But no photograph of Carl," Brook said, finding it difficult to believe that the man had been able to go half of his life without having his picture taken. "Do me a favor and look into Jason Bracco."

"The busboy at the bar and grill?"

"Yes. He hasn't been at work for two days. I had initially thought that maybe he was one of the Swilling brothers, but according to the bartender, Jason was raised in Crestlake. Oh, and run background checks on all the employees at the bar and grill who haven't worked there in past years. Extend that to the pub in town, as well as the coffee shop across from the boutique."

Brook's ringtone interrupted their conversation. She pulled her cell out of her pocket and opened the case. Agent Tirelli's name appeared on the display.

"Sloane."

"It's Tirelli." His loud sigh summed up his reason for calling. "We're running in circles here. No one in Reggie Hollins' life fits your profile."

"Sylvie and Theo might be onto something, but we won't know until later today." Brook pulled her phone away from her face and noted the time. She then pressed the device against her ear. "Are you driving back today? Stop at the lake house and we'll catch you up on our end."

"It will probably be after eight."

"Then meet us at the pub in town," Brook said before disconnecting the call. She walked across the room and tucked her phone in her purse. "Bit, I'm going to drive to Mack Swilling's place. We'll see what he has to say about his middle son. With any luck, he'll have a picture."

"I'll text you the guy's address."

Brook could hear him tapping the keys on his keyboard. As she secured the strap of her purse over her shoulder, a chime alerted her that she had already received the information.

"Aren't you gonna eat before you head out?"

Bit's concern was genuine.

"Enjoy both meals, Bit. I'll grab something on the road." Brook strode to the door, picking up the keys that she had placed on the table. She paused as her hand rested on the worn brass knob. "Something feels...I don't know. We're close. The pieces are there."

"Between you talking with Mack Swilling and Little T honing in on Mitch Swilling, something has to give," Bit said, wiping his fingers on another napkin. "I'll keep you posted, Boss."

"Meet me and Tirelli at the pub around eight."

Brook stepped outside, shutting the door behind her. She pulled her sunglasses down to settle on the bridge of her nose. The clouds were dispersing overhead, and the sun's rays were finally free to illuminate the area. She likened the scenario to her profile. The answers were there in fine print. All that was needed was a little light to guide them.

Chapter Twenty-Five

Theo Neville

May 2024

Monday — 1:54 pm

THEO HAD PARKED THE black SUV across the street from Ricky Austry's apartment. The windows were rolled down to allow a light breeze to cross through over the front seats bringing with it the delicious scents from a local pizzeria. Theo had picked up a protein shake from the hospital's cafeteria earlier this morning, but he could definitely eat some lunch right about now.

The hospital footage that he had combed through this morning had yielded nothing of importance. The only two people who had visited Sheila Wallace during the three days that she had been on life support were Andrea Simpson and Tyler Doss. Seeing as Doss worked for a car dealership, Bit had called them to confirm that Doss had been working on the dates in question. Even without verification, it would have been close to impossible for Doss to take off weeks at a time to observe the victims' daily routines.

Theo caught sight of Sylvie navigating the cracked sidewalk with an effortless grace. Her stride was confident. There was no indication that her injuries hadn't healed properly. She also wasn't hesitant to throw herself into the case.

"Thought you could use this," Sylvie said, offering up a steaming cup of coffee as she slid into the passenger seat. She kept ahold of the other cup, which was most likely a Chai tea. "So, I spoke to the barista. She said that Ricky is a regular, and she also recognized Mitch's picture."

"Was she able to describe Carl?" Theo asked as he removed the white lid to allow his coffee to cool down. He leaned forward and set the plastic disc on the dashboard. "I keep coming back to Tyler Doss, but logistically, he wouldn't have been able to commit those murders. Also, why mention that he believes Mitch is still in contact with Shane Dawkins?"

"The barista said that she has been working at the coffee shop for over a year, and she doesn't recall Ricky being with anyone named Carl. I think Tyler might have just made an assumption. The two men aren't close, but I think it's because Doss might have feelings for Andrea."

"And Andrea has feelings for Mitch."

"Yes." Sylvie adjusted her black-rimmed glasses before shifting in her seat so that she had a better view of the entrance to Austry's apartment building. "No sign of Mitch?"

"None." Theo took a tentative sip of his coffee. It was still too hot to drink, but he did so anyway, liking the bold flavor. "I spoke to Bit. Brook is driving out to Mack Swilling's place. She is hoping that he has a picture of Carl. Worst case scenario, she can get a description."

"She might not have to if we locate Mitch first." Sylvie's phone began to ring, and she reached down into her purse to retrieve it. "It's Dawkins."

A passerby walking down the sidewalk glanced twice in their direction. Her interest had nothing to do with why two individuals were sitting in the vehicle and everything to do with Theo's black eye patch. He shot her a smile, but she had quickly averted her attention.

One of the reasons that he liked Mia so much was that she wasn't bothered by his handicap. It wasn't in her nature to judge people. She was more interested in their life stories.

"Mr. Dawkins, I appreciate your call back," Sylvie said before lowering her phone and switching to speakerphone. "Fortunately, one of your coworkers was able to send us the additional documents. Just so you are aware, I have you on speakerphone. I'm with my colleague, Theo Neville."

"Sandra explained that she spoke to your firm earlier today." Fred's voice came across loud and clear. "I don't know why all the files didn't get attached to the first email. My apologies."

"Mr. Dawkins, the report claimed that you weren't able to find a foster home that would take all three boys," Theo said as he shifted with a subtle lean forward. "Mitch Swilling was sixteen years of age at the time. Do you know if Mitch tried to get custody of them when he turned eighteen?"

"Not to my knowledge, but Ricky had been placed in a really good home. The Austrys adopted him shortly after he turned fourteen."

"And Carl?"

"Well, Carl was the middle boy. He acted out, got into trouble a lot, and honestly, it was a miracle he didn't end up behind bars like his father. If it hadn't been for my friendships in the police department, Carl would have been sent to juvie before his eighteenth birthday."

"Sheila Wallace wouldn't take all three boys?"

"As I shared with Ms. Deering the other day, I did my best to only place older children in her home...those who were independent. Not the young ones who needed help."

"Do you know if they keep in touch?" Sylvie asked before resting her cup on her knee. "Either back then or after Mitch turned eighteen? Maybe Mitch didn't go for custody, but it has come to our attention that Mitch checks in on Ricky from time to time."

"Sure. They would all end up at the youth center together almost every weekend. Ricky's adoptive parents didn't want him to feel as though he couldn't have a relationship with his biological brothers." There was a long pause, but Fred spoke before Theo or Sylvie could ask another question. "Were you able to find Shane?"

Theo noticed that Sylvie closed her eyes in response to Fred's question. The truth of the matter was that Shane had fallen through the cracks. A college dropout who had opted to live on the streets. It was clear that there was more to the story, but Theo doubted that they would ever truly know the facts. Their one goal was to determine whether Shane was their unsub, but that seemed more unlikely with each piece of information revealed.

"No," Sylvie replied softly as she glanced toward Theo. He shook his head, having no other questions for the man. "If that changes, we'll let you know."

"My wife and I would appreciate that very much, Ms. Deering."

As Sylvie ended the call, she groaned before taking a sip of her Chai tea. She let the phone rest on her leg.

"We don't know what Shane's home life was like, Sylvie," Theo reminded her before scanning those near the glass doors of the apartment building. "For all we know, the man changed his name and is living on the West Coast."

"Shane could also be lying in a morgue somewhere," Sylvie muttered as she set her Chai tea in the cup holder. "It must be horrible to not know what happened to your only child. With everything bad that my father did in his life, I'm glad that I was there at his bedside when he died."

Sylvie straightened and pointed in the direction directly in front of them. Theo followed her gaze and locked onto Mitch Swilling as he used the crosswalk to get to the other side of the street. The reason why Theo and Sylvie hadn't driven to Ricky's place of work was out of concern that he would tip off Mitch. Should that happen, both brothers might go underground.

"You cut Swilling off by the apartment building, and I'll come in from behind," Sylvie instructed as she reached for the door handle. Theo had already pressed the button to roll up the windows. "Give me a few seconds to reach the crosswalk."

Sylvie was out of the SUV before the windows were sealed shut. Theo stored his coffee next to her tea in the console before removing the keys from the engine. He monitored Sylvie's progress, and when she made it to the crosswalk, he opened his door. He waited for a lull in traffic before jogging across the street.

Mitch was on his phone, and he wasn't paying attention to his surroundings. As a matter of fact, he seemed annoyed with whoever he was speaking with, though Theo was too far away to hear the man's side of the conversation.

"Excuse me," Theo murmured when he almost bumped into another man.

Mitch's strides faltered when he spotted the firearm holstered to Theo's belt. With the warmer weather, he wasn't able to conceal his weapon, which was why he had taken to hooking the black case securing his credentials next to his holster. Mitch's eyes narrowed in suspicion, but it was when he glanced over his shoulder and spotted Sylvie boxing him in from behind that Mitch told the person on the phone that he would have to call back.

"Whatever it is, I've got nothing to say," Mitch declared, directing his statement more to Sylvie than Theo. She finally came to a stop next to Theo now they were confident Mitch wouldn't make a run for it. "Andrea called me an hour ago to let me know you think I killed those women named Mary Jane Reynolds. I didn't."

"When was the last time you spoke to Carl?"

The way Mitch's head whipped toward Theo after hearing the question was confirmation they were on the right track.

"I haven't seen my brother in over a year."

"About the time that Sheila Wallace died?" Sylvie asked, her tone soft. "Mitch, I know about the room underneath the staircase. I know that Sheila—"

"You're barking up the wrong tree, Agent Deering."

"You kept in touch with your brothers the entire time you were in foster care, and I'm guessing that you called them when you got word that Sheila Wallace was placed on life support," Theo said as he picked up where Sylvie had left off. There wasn't a chance in hell that Mitch would reveal what punishments Sheila had doled out back then, and Theo couldn't blame the man. The mental abuse of a woman like Sheila Wallace stayed with a child into adulthood. "You mentioned that she was an organ donor to your brothers, didn't you? Ricky has solid alibis for the murders, but you don't. Neither does Carl."

"I didn't kill anyone."

"Can you say the same for your brother?" Sylvie asked, softening her tone. "If you can, then tell us where to find him. Once he provides us with alibis for the dates in question, we won't bother any of you again."

Mitch remained silent.

"If you spoke to Andrea, then you know what has happened over the past seven months." Sylvie was still attempting to gain Mitch's cooperation, but the man's body language suggested that he had already made up his mind. Theo realized there was nothing that they could do to change the outcome of this conversation. "There is a very good possibility that another woman is going to die in the near future, Mitch. And all because she was gifted a heart. Shouldn't something good come from that woman?"

"I want a lawyer."

Chapter Twenty-Six

Brooklyn Sloane

May 2024

Monday — 2:49 pm

THE AFTERNOON SUN CAST a pallid light over the decrepit trailer park. The corrosion of time was evident in every rusted panel and dirt-streaked window. Debris cluttered the small yards, some even with hubcaps and tires that had long ago parted ways with their vehicles. Unfortunately, some of the garbage appeared to have become a permanent part of the landscape.

Brook's gaze lingered on one trailer in particular.

She sat motionless in the car, the engine's quiet purr blending in with the vehicles driving on the single-lane road running parallel with the trailer park. It wasn't that the area was busy, but there did seem to be enough of a constant stream of traffic to be an annoyance to those who lived in the mobile homes.

The small gravel area in front of Mack Swilling's trailer was void of any vehicle. The same went for a lot of the other trailers, save for the lone woman some distance away. She was maybe in her sixties, dutifully watering two struggling plants. A broken-down airstream was positioned directly across the single lane. A curtain shifted slightly when her gaze landed on the thin window.

Brook turned off the engine before reaching for her phone that she had placed in the cupholder. She tucked it into the exterior pocket of her blazer before opening the driver's side door. There was a faint odor of fresh-cut grass, but she couldn't hear any lawnmowers in the distance.

The two wooden steps leading up to the trailer door creaked ominously under her weight. She noted the splintering edges and the way the once-white paint had peeled away to reveal the rotting wood underneath. Curtains hung limp just inside the interior door's window. The fabric was so thin that even the weak sunlight seemed too much for them.

Unsurprised by the silence that met her first knock, she rapped on the door again, louder. It was more for show than anything else. No one answering would allow her to make her way across the narrow road to ask the neighbor some questions.

"Anyone home?" Brook called out loudly, her voice carrying on the slight breeze.

With her work at the door done, she descended the steps that miraculously held firm before walking toward the airstream. If the rust on the hubcaps were anything to go by, the tires had deflated long ago. A slab of concrete had been placed right underneath the entrance.

The door flung open, revealing an older man in his seventies or eighties. It was difficult to gauge given his weathered skin. His face was essentially a roadmap of what not to do with one's life, along with a single missing tooth on top and two below. A bottle of beer was in his hand, but he must have already drunk the contents. He was currently using the bottle as a spit container.

"Whatcha want?"

"I'm looking for Mack or Carl Swilling," Brook asked as she removed her sunglasses. She held them in her left hand, along with the car keys. "Do you know if they are at work?"

According to Bit, Mack Swilling appeared to be between jobs. His last position had been working in a warehouse. The company had laid off a few workers, and he had been one of them.

"Who's askin'?" The suspicion in the man's voice was palpable.

Brook took a moment to consider her next move carefully. If she displayed her credentials, he would more than likely slam the door in her face. She decided on a half-truth. The added weight of honesty would help balance the omission.

"There was a death in the family, and I need to speak with them." Brook compressed her lips as if she were contemplating sharing more information, but finally gave a slight shrug instead. "It's personal. I'm sure you can understand, Mr..."

"Puckett. Everyone calls me Puck." Behind him, the interior of the airstream was dimly lit, cluttered, and reeked of sweat. The odor ventured out with every movement, which was often given the man's propensity to spit in the bottle. "Mack ain't been around for a couple of weeks. He got a job with a crew headed down south. A death, you say?"

"Yes. I'm also looking for Mitch Swilling. He is Mr. Swilling's oldest son."

"Never heard of 'em."

"And Carl?" Brook pressed now that Puck was in a talkative state.

"Ain't seen him around, neither." Puck leaned his shoulder against the thin doorway. He studied her vehicle for a moment, and she was glad that her blazer covered her weapon. He might have initially suspected she was with law enforcement, but he appeared content with his own appraisal. "Not since last summer."

"Well, that makes my job a little harder, doesn't it?" Brook said with a touch of frustration as she continued to play her part. "Is Carl the one with the beard? Or is that Ricky?"

"Only Swillings around here are Mack and Carl. Don't know the other two." Puck lifted the bottle to his thin, cracked lips and let his dark saliva drip inside the neck. "And Carl ain't got no beard. At least, he didn't the last time I saw him. Got himself a big ol' tattoo on his right calf, though. Looks more like a three-headed snake than any type of dragon, if you ask me. Is this about some inheritance?"

"It's best I share the news with the Swillings, Puck." Brook lifted a hand and stepped back. "I appreciate your time. I think I'll slip a note inside their door. They can give me a call when one of them returns."

Brook's heels crunched on the gravel as she made her way back to the rental car. She hadn't heard Puck close his door, so she feigned collecting a piece of paper and pen. She sat for a moment, scribbling nonsense until she had counted to fifteen. Figuring that was enough time, she slid the pen back into her purse.

Puck remained rooted in his doorway. She eventually shut the driver's side door before making her way once more toward the rotted steps. The wood was soft and weak beneath her, and she prayed she didn't fall through as the short planks protested her weight. She swung open the screened door, if one could call it that. The mesh had been torn in multiple places and now hung by mere threads on the left side.

Brook went through the motions of leaving a note tucked inside the interior door, though in reality, she did no such thing. By the time she made sure the screened door had latched properly, Puck had already retreated inside his airstream. She didn't waste time and managed to have Bit on the other end of the line before she was settled behind the steering wheel.

"Bit, I need a warrant for Mack Swilling's trailer," Brook stated, knowing full well that such a request would be difficult to attain. "Carl Swilling stays with his father on and off, according to one of the neighbors. Do we have anything that might entice a judge to grant our request?"

"Doubtful," Bit replied hesitantly. "Unfortunately, Big T and Little T hit a wall with Mitch. He won't talk to them, and he even threatened to lawyer up. They are heading over to Ricky's workplace."

Brook tapped her thumb on the steering wheel as she thought over their options. She didn't want to be here all night, but she also didn't want to leave the trailer without some type of surveillance.

"This town has a sheriff, so I'm going to drive over there to see if he can have a deputy park across from the mobile home entrance." Brook paused to think over her options, but there was only one. "Once I'm done at the station, I'll head back. Oh, one more thing. I was told that Carl Swilling has a large tattoo on his right calf—a three-headed dragon. According to a neighbor, it resembles a three-headed snake. If I happen to see a tattoo parlor in town, I'll stop by, but Swilling could have gotten it anywhere. I—"

"A three-headed dragon?"

"Yes," Brook responded as she stopped tapping her thumb. "Why?"

"Give me a minute."

Brook took the time to start the car. She pressed the button to roll down her window. Her presence seemed to have drawn the attention of the woman watering her plants, and she made no effort to hide her curiosity.

"Boss, the hospital gave us that additional footage. There was a male subject with a three-headed dragon on his right calf entering the hospital on the day that Sheila Wallace was taken off life support. He was wearing cargo shorts, but he also had on a hoodie. I'm watching the footage now, but he didn't get off on Wallace's floor. It's the reason that we didn't think anything of his presence. Since I don't have footage from the other floors, I can't follow his movements."

"We have enough for both warrants now. Make it five—include the residences of Ricky Austry, Andrea Simpson, and Tyler Doss. One of them has to be in possession of Carl's photograph. Have Arden put in for the warrants while you see if any traffic cams near the hospital can help you identify Carl Swilling. In the meantime, I'll work on getting a better description of the man," Brook said as she kept her attention on the woman who was now smoking a cigarette. "Let Theo and Sylvie know they can officially bring Mitch and Ricky Swilling in for questioning. They can coordinate the details with the local police."

"On it, Boss."

Brook disconnected the call before closing the driver's side window. Once the glass was sealed, she turned off the engine. Puck was almost certainly watching her every move, but it wouldn't matter in the coming hours. With a warrant in hand, Brook would be accessing Mack Swilling's trailer. With any luck, she would locate a picture of his son and be able to make an official arrest before sunset.

Chapter Twenty-Seven

Brooklyn Sloane

May 2024

Monday — 7:44 pm

A STEADY RAIN HAD turned the day into a murky twilight. The gray curtain had begun to fall relentlessly about six o'clock. By the time Brook had finished up at the trailer park and gotten back on the road, she had cut her usual speed limit by around fifteen miles per hour. Still, she had made it to the pub with time to spare.

The lack of thunder or lightning lent an eerie stillness to the evening, broken only by the rhythmic patter of water on the pavement. She made her way through the downpour, mindful of puddles as the umbrella kept her top half somewhat dry. It was difficult to navigate when the rain was coming at her at an angle.

Brook had already determined that Bit hadn't arrived at the pub before her. The tech van wasn't in sight. While the black vehicle tended to blend in on a busy street, it was also easy to spot if one knew what to search for. There also wasn't an unmarked federal vehicle anywhere in sight, though that wasn't to say Agent Tirelli hadn't driven his personal vehicle.

She opened the door, lowering her umbrella as she stepped inside. Keeping the door ajar, she collapsed the umbrella and shook what remnants of water remained until she was confident that she wouldn't get herself soaking wet by carrying it through the crowd.

For a Monday, the place was quite busy.

Agent Tirelli was nowhere to be found, so she began to scan the room for a table. The bartender raised his hand in greeting. Some of his brown strands were wet, so he must have just arrived for his shift. She nodded back before giving the main area one more passing glance.

Brook finally spotted a high-top with four chairs.

As she carefully weaved her way to the back corner, she hadn't realized how much the rain had dropped the temperature outside. The warmth of the pub was pleasant, and she hoped that the bartender wouldn't mind brewing her up a hot cup of coffee.

Brook claimed the table by pulling out one of the chairs. She then hooked the strap of her purse over the back before tucking her umbrella in the corner. The past few hours had garnered her nothing but a vague description of Carl Swilling—brown hair, brown eyes, and an average build. The only distinctive mark was that of a three-headed dragon tattoo. A search of Mack Swilling's trailer hadn't produced a single photograph.

Using the railing of the chair, Brook settled into the seat. She reached back and pulled her cell phone from the side pocket of her purse. Glancing at the display, she confirmed that Bit hadn't tried to reach her while she had been making her way from the car to the pub. His silence meant that Theo and Sylvie hadn't been successful today, either.

It shouldn't be this difficult to locate an individual in this day and age.

The local police had reached out to a sketch artist who would sit with one of Mack Swilling's neighbors. Such a meeting was taking place now, and the sheriff gave his word that he would email her the electronic drawing first thing. Brook had also spoken with Bit about an aging software program. He stated that he would feed the one photograph that social services had on file into the application and have it run while he met her and Agent Tirelli for dinner.

A sudden vibration garnered her attention. The display on her phone had brightened and revealed Theo's name. She swiped the screen. Pressing the phone to her ear, she realized immediately that she wouldn't be able to hear him over the loud conversations and clinking of glasses.

"Theo, I'm at the pub. I'll call you back when—"

"No, I have..." Theo's voice broke off. "Did you get..."

"Theo, I can't hear you," Brook repeated as she decided to forego the table. Clearly, whatever update Theo wanted to pass on was significant. She stood from the stool, intent on collecting her umbrella and purse when she caught sight of Bit by the entrance. She raised her arm so that he could spot her in the back corner. "Theo, Bit just walked in. Hold on, and I'll go to a quieter area."

"...finally caved and told us that Carl was caught sneaking into Wallace's..."

Bit caught sight of her and began to make his way toward her. He stood out from the other patrons by wearing jeans, a t-shirt that had seen better days, and his knitted hat. Most of the patrons either wore shorts or the clothes that they had worn into the office today.

"...was the one held in that room underneath the..."

"Theo is on the phone, but I can't hear over the noise," Brook said as Bit finally made it to the table. "Please keep an eye on my purse. I'll be right back."

"Boss?" Brook turned back to find that Bit had already hopped onto his seat. "I located Jason Bracco. He is currently in the hospital with a severe case of food poisoning. Severe enough that he's been there for two days."

Brook nodded her understanding before deciding the small hallway near the restrooms was the most ideal place to speak on the phone. If it wasn't pouring rain, she would have taken the call outside. She hadn't made it past two tables when she almost ran into Mindy.

"Excuse me," Brook said as she attempted to edge past the woman.

Fortunately, Cav Buckley wasn't in attendance. Mindy was enjoying a night out with friends, who seemed to be mostly co-workers from the bar and grill. Brook walked past the table, her thoughts switching from Cav to another male subject. She didn't let on that she might have made a connection through mere initials.

C.S.

Coincidence?

Tension settled in Brook's shoulders as she finished crossing the room. When she came to the small hallway, she lifted the cell phone to her ear. The noise from the patrons had become somewhat muted, allowing her to find out what Theo had discovered from Mitch Swilling in Ann Arbor.

"Theo, I'm in a place where I can talk." Brook leaned a shoulder against the wall as she stared at a particular group. She lowered her gaze to one subject's legs in particular, and her adrenaline spiked when she realized that he was wearing shorts. "Bit and I are at the pub, waiting for Tirelli to show up."

"Mitch Swilling finally spoke to us at his lawyer's urging, Brook. We know the identity of our unsub," Theo revealed right as the man whom Brook had in her sights stood from the table. In doing so, he pushed his chair back and took a step in the opposite direction, patting another man on the shoulder in the process. The movement was enough for Brook to get a perfect visual of a three-headed dragon on the exposed skin of his right calf. "Carl Swilling is posing as Chip Schofield. Chip is Mitch Swilling's brother. You'll need to—"

"Chip Schofield is here at the pub, Theo," Brook divulged as she raised her eyes to the back of the man's head. Mindy had placed her hand on his arm, causing him to turn. In doing so, his gaze sought her out. Considering that he had flown under their radar for weeks, she wouldn't have thought anything of it. Now? He stared directly at her, and she was instinctively aware of the shift in his demeanor. "Get ahold of Tirelli. I'll do my best to apprehend Carl Swilling without anyone else getting hurt."

Brook quickly thought over her options. Chip—Carl—stood still and maintained eye contact with her all the while Mindy continued her side of the conversation. He, too, was apparently going over his options. In her peripheral vision, Brook was able to spot Bit as he abruptly stood from the table. Theo must have texted him, and his timing couldn't have been more perfect.

Mary Jane Reynolds had just entered the bar with her sister, both of them laughing loudly enough to capture everyone's attention. Carl slowly smiled, and he hadn't even turned around to verify who had walked through the door. He hadn't needed to from all the observing he had done over the past few weeks.

The air grew heavy with tension, and the noise around Brook faded as she zeroed in on her target. She wasn't keen on drawing her weapon in the middle of a bar, but she would do what was necessary to prevent him from achieving his goal. In all likelihood, he wouldn't care if she shot him dead...as long as he was able to stop Sheila Wallace's heart from beating ever again.

As Mindy chatted away, oblivious to the impending threat, Carl's smile widened into a chilling grin that spoke of his intent. There was a darkness in his eyes that had nothing to do with their color. Brook subtly adjusted her position before tucking her phone into the pocket of her blazer.

Carl discreetly reached for a steak knife on the table next to the other man's plate. He noticed and started to object, but it was too late. Carl's fingers wrapped around the handle of the knife and pulled the sharp blade from the table.

Unaware that she was about to be attacked, Mary Jane continued deeper into the pub with her sister. The federal agent in charge of her safety was two steps behind her, but he had no idea that his subject was about to be attacked from the front.

Brook wouldn't be able to reach Carl in time to stop him, so she was forced to draw her weapon. The women moved closer just as Carl was ready to strike. Mindy finally noticed that Carl had been staring in Brook's direction, but the woman had also spotted the knife in his hand. She backed up a few steps, bumping into the person behind her. It was then that Carl took advantage of the distraction. He raised his arm and used his momentum to swing around, fully intending to plunge the knife into Mary Jane's chest.

Unfortunately, someone stepped in front of Brook at the last minute, forcing her to remove her finger from the trigger. In a swift and unexpected move, Bit made a run for Carl to stop the vicious attack. The sudden disruption knocked Mary Jane back, affording the federal agent the ability to get her to safety while Carl was sent crashing into a table. Glasses shattered, chairs scraped the floor, and everyone scattered as chaos erupted in the bar. Brook pushed forward directing everyone back while Bit grappled with Carl.

Bit wrestled for control of the knife while Carl became somewhat manic. Brook waited for the right moment to step in, but her help wasn't needed. While both men fiercely wrestled one another on the wooden floor, Bit managed to bend Carl's wrist to the point where the man was forced to release the knife. Brook used her heel to kick the weapon out of reach while Bit successfully flipped Carl over and pinned him down, exerting enough force to keep him restrained in a prone position.

Fortunately, Agent Tirelli had materialized with a pair of handcuffs. He held them out for Bit, all the while reassuring the patrons that they would be able to continue with their evening in a few moments. He then leaned down and assisted Bit with pulling Carl into a standing position.

"I want a lawyer."

"I guess this means we're not getting dinner anytime soon," Tirelli muttered to Brook before launching into the Miranda rights as he escorted Carl out of the bar.

By this time, Brook had holstered her weapon and knelt to pick up Bit's grey knitted cap. By the time she had straightened, Bit was leaning over with his hands on his knees. His blond hair hung around his face as he took a moment to draw oxygen into his lungs. Brook couldn't help but reach out and pat his back in praise.

"That was some field work, Bit," Brook commended as he reached up and took his cap. He made no move to put it on as he continued to stay in a bent position. "You saved Mary Jane Reynold's life by putting yourself at risk."

"Just don't go telling Big T that I feel as if I was hit by a Mack Truck." Bit slowly straightened until he was able to adjust his hat in place. His usual pale features were flushed, and beads of sweat had formed on his temples. "He'll try to coerce me into working out with him every morning, and I'm pretty sure that I would die from a stroke or something."

Bit took one last long inhalation before flashing her a smile.

"Was that an epic takedown or what?"

"Epic," Brook agreed with him as she steered him to the corner to grab her purse. While Agent Tirelli would handle the arrest, they would be inundated with paperwork. They also needed to touch base with Theo and Sylvie. First, though, she needed to get Bit a drink. She glanced over her shoulder and held up a hand. The bartender nodded his understanding. "Let's sit for a moment."

"It was the element of surprise," Bit continued as he reached for her umbrella, not taking in her suggestion of sitting at the table. She didn't comment about the tremor in his hand, but she did manage to take the umbrella from him and put it back in the corner. His adrenaline rush was gradually wearing off, and the knowledge that he had put his own life at risk to save another would gradually sink in. "Fast reflexes, you know?"

"I know," Brook said as he finally hopped onto the high-top chair. She reclaimed her seat, ensuring that her purse was still in its place. The patrons had all pitched in and were doing their best to clean up the shattered glass and right the tables and chairs into their upright positions. "You handled the situation like any federal field agent would have in such circumstances. You were closest to the suspect, and you were able to disarm him without anyone getting hurt."

Brook had noticed that Mindy had collected a small garbage bin to help with the cleanup. Her motions were slow, indicating that she was in shock for very different reasons.

"Mindy, would you mind?" Brook held out her hand, prompting Mindy to close the distance between them. She sluggishly handed off the black plastic bin. "Thanks. You'll want to get another one. Trust me."

Mindy tilted her head in confusion, but her name was being called by someone near the table. She finally walked away to help him, leaving Brook alone with Bit. The previous color on his cheeks from the physical exertion was wearing off, and his pallor was now a shade lighter than usual. She lifted the small plastic pail over the table right as he made a declaration.

"Boss? I think I'm going to throw up."

CHAPTER TWENTY-EIGHT

Brooklyn Sloane

May 2024

Tuesday — 10:19 am

THE DARK LIQUID FORMED a perfect swirling stream into the mug. Once the remaining contents were transferred, Brook rinsed out the glass carafe and positioned it safely on the top rack of the dishwasher. A quick survey of the kitchen revealed there was nothing left to clean. The counters had been disinfected, the refrigerator had been cleaned out, and the garbage cans had already been taken to the curb. The only thing left for her to do before she left the lake house was to finish her coffee. She would include her mug in the dishwasher before programming the wash cycle.

"...hate garage sales." Sylvie's voice drifted into the kitchen. She was helping Bit dismantle and store the computer equipment in plastic bins that would then be packed into the back of the tech van. "Why on earth would you have lied like that?"

"It wasn't like I set out to lie to Zoey's mother. You had to be there, Little T. The woman caught me off guard, and I..."

Brook picked up her coffee and walked over to the sliding glass door. Last night's downpour seemed to have transformed the area. The grass glistened in the morning sun, the vivid green a stark contrast to the darker hues of the lake. The water was peaceful this time of day, and there were numerous fishing boats peppered across the surface. She focused on the deck, ensuring that nothing had been left out back. Theo or Bit must have already removed the security camera used to surveil the pier. For good measure, she tugged on the handle to confirm the lock was secure.

"Brook?" Theo had been loading their luggage into the SUV since he had decided to fly back to Washington, D.C. with her. Sylvie would accompany Bit on the drive back home. "We have a couple of visitors."

Brook made her way through the kitchen and into the living room. Standing in the doorway was Mary Jane Reynolds. Her focus was on Bit, who had shifted his weight in discomfort at the attention. His unease became even worse when she rushed over to him and threw her arms around his neck.

"I don't know how to thank you," Mary Jane exclaimed before pulling back. By this time, her fiancé had stepped into the house and closed the door behind him. "All of you."

"I, uh, should probably apologize." Adam glanced at Mary Jane, who arched her brow that he shouldn't just stop there. "I'm sorry if I came on too strong. In hindsight, it probably wasn't the best move to park outside your rental place. I love Mary Jane, and it was extremely hard to stand on the sidelines believing that someone wanted to kill her. Thank you for taking on the investigation and saving her life."

"You were both put in a very difficult situation," Brook said as Adam shook Theo's hand. "As for us taking the case, it was the FBI who reached out to us. Jurisdiction isn't always clear-cut, and this case was unusual. We're just pleased that an arrest was made, and you no longer have to worry about your safety. You should know that I received a call about an hour ago confirming that Carl Swilling's DNA matched the evidence at all three crime scenes."

"I don't know how I feel about..." Mary Jane couldn't finish her sentence, and she rested a hand over her heart.

Her pained facial expression said it all.

"You were given a gift, Mary Jane," Brook said softly. "Whatever Sheila Wallace did or didn't do in her life has no bearing on how you live yours. It's yours now to embrace without fear."

"If your morning post is anything to go by, it sounds as if you're already ahead of the curve." Sylvie was shaking her head at what she had shared with the team earlier. Mary Jane had posted that she and her fiancé had decided to get married before bungee jumping off the Navajo Bridge in Arizona. Personally, Brook couldn't imagine Adam Bouras craving such an adrenaline rush, but Mary Jane appeared to be able to convince him of practically anything. "Bungee jumping? No, thank you."

Mary Jane laughed and held out her hand to Adam, waiting to speak until he was by her side.

"I know what you all thought when you first met me. Why would a woman want to post constantly about her life? But after I received a new heart, I knew I couldn't take it for granted. It might take me a while to come to terms with everything that has happened, especially the realization that my heart came from a woman who wasn't a kind person, but that surgery changed me. It's the reason I share every beautiful moment with the world. I need to document each sacred moment, so decades from now, I'll know...I lived fully."

Brook stood in awe of the woman's courage. A few more pleasantries were exchanged before the team eventually wished the couple well. Theo walked them out, leaving Brook to finish her coffee and Bit to finally snap the lid on the last plastic storage bin.

"I've got to say that I never viewed posting online in quite that way before," Sylvie said as she took a seat on the couch. "Still, I don't think I could use social media as a diary."

"It might be different if we didn't see the consequences of posting our locations, the faces of our friends and family, and our everyday activities on social media for everyone to see." Bit took a seat on the plastic container. There were only a few bins left to pack in the back of the van. "My sister uses social media, but I avoid it like the plague."

"Theo has an account, but he has it limited to family and close friends." Sylvie laughed at Bit's disdained expression. "Theo understands that someone knowing their way around software like you can pretty much access everything. He doesn't post so much as it serves as a way to keep in touch with those who live far away."

"Boss? I bet you would rather bungee jump off the Navajo Bridge than join social media."

Sylvie started to laugh as Brook finished her coffee before turning to walk into the kitchen. They were well-versed in her thoughts on social media. She didn't need to refresh their memory. It didn't take her long to store the mug on the top rack of the dishwasher and press the start button.

"Ready to go?" Theo asked, prompting Brook to glance over her shoulder. He was standing in the archway of the kitchen, holding the keys to the SUV in his hand. "Bit and Sylvie took the last of the bins out to the tech van. All that's left to do is lock up and place the key in the lock box outside."

"Yes. I'm ready to go."

Something fluttered outside the window, catching Brook's attention. A beautiful male cardinal settled on the railing of the wooden deck. The same type of bird that had been in her dream about summer camp a few weeks ago. Maybe she truly had met Stella Bennett back in 1996. With Brook's childhood, she tried not to put too much stock into signs.

Her phone chimed. Pulling the device out of her back pocket, the lighted display alerted her to a message from Special Agent Dever. Her heart rate accelerated as she swiped the notification to the right.

The remains had finally been confirmed to be that of Stella Bennett.

Brook couldn't help but lift her gaze to the magnificent cardinal staring directly at her through the window. Neither one of them moved. Eventually, she needed to breathe and slowly released the air inside her lungs. The bird's response was to spread its bright red wings and fly away.

CHAPTER TWENTY-NINE

Jacob Walsh

May 2024

Friday — 11:12 am

THE FLUORESCENT TUBES BUZZED overhead, the sterile light reflecting off the polished steel surface of the table. The room was basically a cube. It had purposefully been designed to be devoid of comfort. There was no odor whatsoever, and the temperature was neither cold nor warm without a ripple in the air.

All was still.

Jacob had lost count of the number of times that he had been seated in this very spot over the past year. Longer, actually. His days and nights were turning into a monotonous cycle that he had not intended to take place. It had gotten to the point where even his daily shit happened at the same time.

It was obvious that he had underestimated his sister.

Brook had evolved into a formidable adversary. It was a transformation that he would never openly acknowledge. She had always been tenacious, even as a little girl. She couldn't stand not knowing what had made them turn out so differently. He comprehended the basic truth, though—they were much more alike than she was willing to admit.

Another minute had passed, and Jacob still sat immobile in the chair. The handcuffs around his wrists were anchored to the eyehook bolted into the table. The same had been done with the chain between his ankles. Such precautions were insulting, but there was little he could do about it right now. Brook had managed to subvert his objectives to escape federal prison multiple times.

The heavy door finally swung open, but it wasn't his sister who crossed the threshold. Jacob slowly curled his fingers into his fists as his irritation began to morph into rage. He never would have done something so obvious in front of Brook, and the federal prosecutor who had entered the room didn't have the acumen to notice.

"Don't bother sitting." The sharp scent of the man's aftershave left a bad taste in Jacob's mouth. "You can leave."

The prosecutor paused mid-motion, but he eventually placed his briefcase on the table. The wedding band on his finger was wider than the smile on his face as he introduced himself, but Jacob discarded the man's name. There was no need to remember it.

"I'm here to formally charge you with the murder of Stella Bennett. You'll be given time to reach out to your previous legal counsel, hire a new attorney, or be represented by a public—"

"I'm only going to say this once." Jacob's declaration halted the prosecutor midsentence. "If you don't leave this room right now, I will find your wife and peel the flesh from her face in thin strips and mail them to you one by one. And when I'm done with her, I'll start hunting down every woman you've ever fucked. Is your mother still alive?"

The prosecutor was intelligent enough to heed Jacob's warning. The man picked up his briefcase and then walked toward the door. His stride wasn't as graceful as it had been entering the room. He used his fist to bang against the heavy exit to alert the guard on the other side that his time had come to an end.

"Before you decide on legal counsel, you should know that the death penalty will be on the table."

Jacob remained motionless as the man's footsteps receded down the hallway. The guard closed the door, though he would be back momentarily to escort Jacob back to his cell. He rested his palms flat on the cool steel surface of the table to center himself.

Brook hadn't delivered the news herself. It was her way of informing him that she had washed her hands clean of the past. In the time that he had voluntarily put himself behind bars for the purpose of finishing what he started—draining the life from Sarah Evanston's body—his sister had made a feeble attempt at piecing together a life.

Well, it was his turn to send her a message.

Jacob focused on a singular thought that had kept him sane during his incarceration—his fail-safe plan. It was a strategy that he had never expected to use, because he had never allowed himself to believe that Brook would discover Stella Bennett's remains.

Still, he had been wise enough to plan for every contingency.

The prosecutor had been right about one thing. Jacob needed a lawyer, but not just any lawyer. There was only one who could implement a new path. One that led not through a courtroom, but to freedom.

~ The End ~

Dive into the next thrilling installment of the Touch of Evil series by USA Today Bestselling Author Kennedy Layne...

Is anyone ever truly prepared to face the sins of their past?

Jordan Miles, revered CEO of Miles Therapeutics, finds himself at the center of a scandal when he is arrested for his wife's murder. Determined to salvage his reputation and prove his innocence, he turns to the one person he believes can hunt down the real killer.

Enter Brooklyn Sloane, a former FBI profiler who has spent her career tracking serial murderers. While she typically steers clear of ongoing investigations, her personal friendship with Jordan compels her to take the case. The police allege that Jordan shot his wife point blank during an argument in their bedroom, but Brook doesn't believe for a moment that he is guilty. What secrets has his wife taken to her grave?

With the clock ticking and the pressure mounting, Brook warns Jordan that their search for the truth could shatter the illusion of his perfect life. As she and the team peel back the layers of Jordan's seemingly ideal existence, they soon realize the cost of redemption may be higher than they ever dared imagine.

OTHER BOOKS BY KENNEDY LAYNE

The Graveside Mysteries

Twisted Graves
Delicate Graves
Shadowed Graves

The Widow Taker Trilogy

The Forgotten Widow
The Isolated Widow
The Reclusive Widow

Hex on Me Mysteries

If the Curse Fits
Cursing up the Wrong Tree
The Squeaky Ghost Gets the Curse
The Curse that Bites
Curse Me Under the Mistletoe
Gone Cursing

Paramour Bay Mysteries

Magical Blend
Bewitching Blend
Enchanting Blend
Haunting Blend
Charming Blend
Spellbinding Blend
Cryptic Blend
Broomstick Blend
Spirited Blend
Yuletide Blend
Baffling Blend
Phantom Blend
Batty Blend
Pumpkin Blend
Frosty Blend
Stony Blend
Cocoa Blend
Shamrock Blend
Campfire Blend
Stormy Blend
Sparkling Blend
Hallow Blend
Dandelion Blend
Cranberry Blend
Nautical Blend

Office Roulette Series

Means
Motive
Opportunity

Keys to Love Series

Unlocking Fear
Unlocking Secrets
Unlocking Lies
Unlocking Shadows
Unlocking Darkness

Surviving Ashes Series

Essential Beginnings
Hidden Flames
Buried Flames
Endless Flames
Rising Flames

CSA Case Files Series

Captured Innocence
Sinful Resurrection
Renewed Faith
Campaign of Desire
Internal Temptation
Radiant Surrender
Redeem My Heart
A Mission of Love

Red Starr Series

Starr's Awakening
Hearths of Fire
Targets Entangled
Igniting Passion
Untold Devotion
Fulfilling Promises
Fated Identity
Red's Salvation

The Safeguard Series

Brutal Obsession
Faithful Addiction
Distant Illusions
Casual Impressions

Honest Intentions
Deadly Premonitions

ABOUT THE AUTHOR

Kennedy Layne, a USA Today bestselling author, resides in the Midwest with her retired Marine Master Sergeant husband and their menagerie of pets. Fueled by coffee and her love for thrillers, cozy mysteries, and romantic suspense novels, Kennedy loves to spend time in front of her fireplace crafting stories that keep her readers guessing until the very end.

Email:

kennedylayneauthor@gmail.com

Facebook:

facebook.com/kennedy.layne.94

Twitter:

twitter.com/KennedyL_Author

Website:

www.kennedylayne.com

Newsletter:

www.kennedylayne.com/meet-kennedy.html

Made in United States
Orlando, FL
05 June 2025

61834501R10134